How could one man feel so safe?

Her breathing calmed, her pulse no longer thundered in her ears. But she wasn't budging. For the first time in two days, Brooke felt normal again. She wasn't afraid. She was just… a woman.

He was hard in the places she was soft— muscled through the chest and arms, growing leaner down to his waist.

Then Atticus leaned back, easing some space between them. He stroked her jaw with the backs of his fingers. "Better?"

JULIE MILLER

ARMED AND DEVASTATING

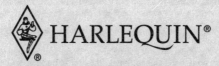

HARLEQUIN®

TORONTO • NEW YORK • LONDON
AMSTERDAM • PARIS • SYDNEY • HAMBURG
STOCKHOLM • ATHENS • TOKYO • MILAN • MADRID
PRAGUE • WARSAW • BUDAPEST • AUCKLAND

For Ryne Scott Miller. Congratulations on your graduation.
You've had a stellar career in so many ways, and have a
great future ahead of you. You're funny. You have great
friends. And you're a nice guy, to boot. I'm proud of all your
accomplishments in music and science and Scouts and more.
But mostly, I'm just proud of the fine man you are. I love you
more than you may ever know. Mushy enough for you?

Mom

Thanks to Polly Revare and her family for inviting us to stay
in their gorgeous remodeled church home.

ISBN-13: 978-0-373-69340-5
ISBN-10:   0-373-69340-0

ARMED AND DEVASTATING

Copyright © 2008 by Julio Millor

www.eHarlequin.com

Printed in U.S.A.

ABOUT THE AUTHOR

Julie Miller attributes her passion for writing romance to all those fairy tales she read growing up, and shyness. Encouragement from her family to write down all those feelings she couldn't express became a love for the written word. She gets continued support from her fellow members of the Prairieland Romance Writers, where she serves as the resident "grammar goddess." This award-winning author and teacher has published several paranormal romances. Inspired by the likes of Agatha Christie and Encyclopedia Brown, Ms. Miller believes the only thing better than a good mystery is a good romance.

Born and raised in Missouri, she now lives in Nebraska with her husband, son and smiling guard dog, Maxie. Write to Julie at P.O. Box 5162, Grand Island, NE 68802-5162.

Books by Julie Miller

CAST OF CHARACTERS

Atticus Kincaid—A by-the-book cop obsessed with finding the truth about his father's murder. But after Brooke Hansford is targeted by a sicko secret admirer, Atticus throws the rule book out the window—and starts protecting more than just his investigation.

Brooke Hansford—A shy plain Jane who may hold the key to several murders. If only she knew what that key was and where it was hidden. As events in her life grow stranger and more dangerous, will she transform herself into an assertive, confident she-warrior who can meet the threats head-on?

Penny and Louise Hansford—The aunts who raised Brooke.

Tony Fierro—The handyman.

Mirza Patel—A friend from assertiveness training class.

Kevin Grove—Homicide detective.

William Caldwell—A Kincaid family friend who may be next on a mysterious hit list.

Leo Hansford—The father Brooke never knew. He gave his life and his heart for his country.

Deputy Commissioner John Kincaid—His unsolved murder haunts his four sons.

Chapter One

"And I shall hear, tho' soft you tread above me…"

Detective Atticus Kincaid pushed his white handkerchief into his mother's icy hand and wrapped an arm around her trembling shoulders.

Susan Kincaid was holding up like a rock through her husband's funeral service and burial ceremony, but Atticus could sense a brittleness to her stoic composure. And even through the raincoat she wore, he felt a chill that he suspected had as much to do with the shock and emptiness inside as it did with the rain beating down on the green awning over their heads and misting the air around them.

"Your father loved this song," she whispered, scarcely loud enough for him to hear. She wrung the handkerchief between her fingers, catching Atticus's hand and holding on tight. "Holden sounds so much like him when he sings it."

"He sure does," Atticus agreed, sitting ramrod-straight and allowing his mother to take whatever strength she needed from him. Dutifully, he turned his attention back to his younger brother, who stood beside their father's flag-draped casket, singing Deputy Commissioner John Kincaid's favorite song.

"…sleep in peace until you come to me."

Damned ironic. His father was a good cop. A great man. The best father any four sons could ask for. There was nothing peaceful about the idea of some unknown perps kidnapping and torturing him, and then shooting him at point-blank range. How could John Kincaid rest in peace when his killer was out there somewhere, not giving a damn about the pain he was causing this family? Maybe even gloating at the huge hole John Kincaid's death left in the ranks of the Kansas City Police Department?

Was the motive personal? Professional?

Why were the clues collected from the crime scene so sketchy? Why were there no suspects in custody? Why the hell didn't homicide already have a man behind bars for this travesty?

Atticus's skin crawled with the need to find answers.

But for right now, he'd sit here amongst the gathering of family, friends and fellow cops, and pretend he had everything under control—for his mother's sake.

Holden finished the song, placed his KCPD hat back on his head and raised a white-gloved hand to salute their father. Atticus pressed his own hand over the Kansas City Police Department badge clipped to the pocket of his dark-blue dress uniform, feeling the black mourning ribbon beneath his palm like the slash of a knife straight through the heart that lay beneath. But a hand over his heart was the only outward sign of grief he allowed himself to show.

He heard a noisy sniffle behind his right shoulder and

glanced up to see his father's administrative assistant, Brooke Hansford, wiping away the tears beneath her thick, owl-like glasses. Brooke had been his father's organizational and technological savior at work. And though he'd always figured she was about his age—thirty—she looked young and fragile and completely vulnerable with her pale cheeks and red-tipped nose.

Lacking a second handkerchief to give her, Atticus waited until her puffy gaze met his and he offered her a wink. Brooke responded with a hasty smile and a loud sniff before ducking her head to dig into her oversize purse—for a tissue, no doubt.

Yeah. The bastard who'd killed John Kincaid had robbed a lot of good people of someone they loved.

The minister was saying a last few words, but checking on Brooke had already diverted Atticus's attention to the other mourners surrounding them. He spotted his older brother, Sawyer, standing hatless in the rain, his anger and grief evident in the grim expression on a face that was normally creased with a smile. He was shifting from foot to foot, restlessly scanning the crowd as he listened to the graying man standing beside him. Though a black umbrella obscured part of his face, William Caldwell, one of their father's oldest friends, was easily recognized by the expensive tailoring of his suit and coat and the gold fraternity ring that matched the one his father had been buried with.

A lot of people were hurting today.

Atticus absorbed each flinch of his mother's hand as the honor guard sounded off their twenty-one-gun salute. But he barely heard the explosive pops himself as he swung his gaze around to find one more family member.

It wasn't until his mother clasped the folded flag to her chest and he stood beside her that Atticus finally located his oldest brother, Edward, standing beneath a canopy of pine boughs and budding ash branches, some thirty yards from the main group. Edward seemed to be leaning heavily on his cane, but his chin was held high, and he looked a hell of a lot more put together than the last time Atticus had seen him.

Susan Kincaid squeezed Atticus's arm. She'd seen her oldest child, too. "Go talk to him, will you, son? I don't want Edward to think he's all alone at a time like this."

Edward had chosen to be alone for months now, but today wasn't the day to point out that fact. "Yes, ma'am." He nodded to Holden to take his place at their mother's side. "Holden?"

"I'll stick with her." Holden drew her hand into the crook of his arm.

"You did a beautiful job, sweetie." As Susan stretched up to kiss her youngest son's cheek, Atticus pulled down the brim of his KCPD hat and picked up an umbrella to do her bidding.

He wasted no time cutting straight across the sloping hill. Edward might have become a pro at hiding out in a shadowy house or the bottom of a bottle, but no way could he outrun his determined brother. The master detective's shield Edward had locked away might outrank Atticus's own detective's badge, but as far as he was concerned, their mom outranked them all. And if she wanted someone to bring Edward back into the family fold, then, by damn, Atticus was going to do it.

Edward's gray eyes, one of the few things they seemed to have in common these days, scowled at Atticus's out-stretched hand.

But stubbornness was another shared trait. "Don't tell me you don't recognize what this means, Edward. It's good to see you."

His oldest brother seemed to need time to process what the gesture of man-to-man friendship might cost him. But then perhaps he remembered which brother could go the longest before saying "uncle" in one of their childhood backyard pile-on tussling matches. Atticus was relieved to feel the firmness of Edward's grip when he finally reached out to shake his hand. "Don't you dare try to hug me."

Atticus's mouth curved with half a laugh. He shifted to stand beside his brother and watch the distant pomp and grieving from his lonely perspective. Maybe the silence should have been awkward. But Edward had never been much of a talker. The soft patter of the rain on the overhanging branches was a soothing sound in the quiet, and the deep scent of the wet pine surrounding them reminded Atticus of saner, happier times when their father had taken the boys camping and fishing on weekend trips.

But the sweet memories of all they had lost began to curdle in Atticus's stomach, and the solace of the moment passed. Since Edward hadn't yet bolted for cover, Atticus carried out their mother's request. "You should come say hi to Mom. She knows you're here, but it'd mean a hell of a lot to her if you made the effort to touch base." He glanced over at Edward, who rested both hands on the grip of his cane now. "She's hurting. We all are."

"I don't hurt anymore." The words rolled out with a dark note of finality. Maybe he'd been in pain for so long that he was done feeling anything. Was it respect alone that had made him get out of bed and trim his beard and get here this afternoon? Edward tilted his thick walnut cane and pointed toward the green awning. "But this pisses me off."

So big brother felt something, after all.

There was more silence as the crowd began to disperse, opening umbrellas and turning up collars as they walked down the hill to the cars lining the road that twisted through Mount Washington Cemetery. Finally, Edward pulled back his shoulders and turned to Atticus with a gut-deep sigh. "I'm sure Mom has invited people over to the house, but I can't do the small-talk thing. Just give her my love."

"Give it to her yourself. Let me get Sawyer and Holden on this. We'll keep everyone away and you can have a private moment with her before she leaves Mount Washington."

Edward thought hard about the offer, then nodded.

"You know, Ed, if you ever need anything—"

"Don't go there." A muscle ticked beneath the scar slashing along Edward's jaw. "I'll meet you by her car in ten minutes." He limped away from the crowd, pausing at the far edge of the copse of trees. He never turned back around. "Thanks, A. It's good to see you, too."

The gruff admission may have been the truest comfort Atticus had had since learning of their father's murder several days earlier. But the reprieve was over. With the hardest part of his mission accomplished, Atticus easily spotted Sawyer, standing a head taller than anyone else in the crowd, and went to make the arrangements for the meeting.

He was on track to find Holden and their mother when a smooth feminine voice purred behind him. "Atticus." Familiar white-tipped nails clutched the sleeve of his jacket, stopping him. Atticus braced as a blond-haired woman lowered her umbrella and stepped into view. Every silvery-gold strand was perfectly placed around her striking features, every word was carefully chosen. "I'm so sorry this had to happen to you—to your family."

"Hayley." He couldn't help but check to see if her cameraman was trailing behind her. Despite the male escort he didn't recognize standing back at a polite distance, she appeared to be unplugged. *Say something nice.* After all, those could be tears, not raindrops glistening on her cheeks. "Thanks for coming."

"Your father was a valuable asset to the police department. He was always good about keeping the lines of communication open with the press. He raised four wonderful sons, as well. I admired him." The nails dug in as Hayley Resnick tipped her lips up to kiss him.

Uh-uh. He couldn't do this. Not today of all damn days. Atticus turned his head, and after the briefest of pauses, she settled for pressing a kiss to his cheek. "How's your mother doing?"

Atticus resisted the impulse to bolt when she released him to open her umbrella again. He didn't want the woman he'd once bought an engagement ring for to think she could still trigger that kind of emotional response in him. He'd confused her desire for an urbane escort, a willing lover— and an inside source for KCPD information—with love. He wouldn't make that same mistake again. He could play the same pretend-I-give-a-damn game if she could. "Mom's holding her own. Exhausted. Not eating like she should. About as well as can be expected."

"I'm sorry to hear that. Will there be a gathering at the house? I'd like to pay my respects—"

"No," he lied. Too quickly. *Keep your cool, Kincaid.*

"Just the immediate family and a few close friends from work. Like I said, Mom's pretty worn out."

His family's grief was a private thing. He'd learned the hard way that Hayley wasn't above using pillow talk to ferret out a story and further her career. She'd never quoted him directly, hadn't legally broken the boundaries between free speech and police security, but there wasn't an offhand comment that she couldn't turn into a lead if she sensed there was a story to be had. Atticus needed to end this conversation before the reporter in her picked up on some nuance of intonation, and she detected just how close to the surface his pain and frustrations were riding.

And then he spotted the perfect excuse to walk away. Brooke Hansford, heading down to the road, slipped on the wet grass. That big hobo bag swung out, nearly dragging her to the ground before she caught herself. Wiping her wet and probably muddy hand on her coat, she glanced quickly around. Her soggy bun bounced against her neck as she checked to make sure no one had seen the gaffe. When her eyes met his, she froze for a moment. But then she pushed her glasses up on her nose, stuffed her hands into her pockets and turned away. Even at this distance, she couldn't hide the rosy blush that stained her cheeks.

The tension eased from the clench of his jaw, due as much to Brooke's ingenuous embarrassment as to the easy opportunity she presented. Atticus summoned the practiced smile that had carried him throughout the day. "If you'll excuse me. I see a friend I need to catch up with. Again, thanks for coming."

It felt good to leave with the last word for a change.

Lengthening his stride, Atticus angled down the hill and quickly caught up with Brooke. He adjusted his umbrella over her head and fell into step beside her. "Need a lift to the house? Mom said you were helping with the pot luck."

All he could see was the part in her curly, blond-brown hair as she kept her eyes glued to the path in front of her. "Um, no thanks. I have my car."

He followed the point of her finger to the blue VW Beetle about a quarter mile down the road. "Then let me walk you there so you don't get soaked to the skin."

"You don't have to—"

"Dad would have my hide if I let a lady walk that far in the rain without benefit of a hat or umbrella." To show Brooke that he wasn't taking no for an answer, Atticus tugged on her wrist, pulling her hand from her pocket and linking her arm through his.

Hayley had grabbed as if she still had the right. Brooke paused, looked at her mud-dappled hand where it hovered over his sleeve, and finally, with a sniffle that probably had as much to do with the mention of John Kincaid as with the chilly dampness, she lightly curled her fingers into the material and nodded. "Okay."

Atticus was a cop as much as he was a hurting man. He'd just said his amens and put his slain father in the ground. Though he knew protocol wouldn't allow him to work the murder investigation, something needed to be done. Besides, work was a hell of a lot easier to focus on than any grief or resentment he might feel. "What was Dad working on before he left the office last week?"

Turning the conversation to work, Brooke seemed to relax. Her hand rested more naturally on his arm and she began to talk. "Paperwork mostly. He was clearing his desk, moving from task force captain to deputy commissioner. You know—writing final reports, passing open cases on to other precincts, briefing the watch commanders. He was working on his memoirs, too. Journaling—making a record of his career highlights, I guess. He wouldn't let me transcribe any of that—said it was personal, not police business."

"Do you have some free time in the next few days that we could go over that stuff?"

"Sure, I've got the time. But homicide collected most of his files. You might have better luck talking to Detective Grove. He's heading up the investigation. I'm not sure what I'd actually be able to access for you."

Grove. Brooke had already provided more information on the case than he'd had a minute ago. Atticus didn't know Kevin Grove well, other than that he'd come over from the cold case division a couple of years back and had a reputation as an experienced investigator.

Still, Atticus wasn't ready to leave justice up to a relative stranger. "Anything might help. Are you willing to try?"

"For your dad, sure. I can't understand why anyone would want to hurt him."

Atticus killed the conversation with his bleak pronouncement. "He was a cop for thirty years, Brooke. The man was bound to make some enemies."

Her grip stiffened on his sleeve and they reached the asphalt before she spoke again. "I miss your dad. The office seems so empty without his laugh or his grousing at the computer when it doesn't do what he wants it to. John always said he just wanted to turn on the computer and have it work. He didn't want to learn all the tricks and shortcuts, said that's what I was for."

Atticus ducked his head, catching a glimpse of a wistful smile before her eyes met his and widened behind her rain-spotted glasses and she glanced away. He straightened, nodded to a passing driver, and guided her across the road. "Dad always said you were his right hand at work. If he couldn't find a file, you knew where it was. If a case had him all worked up, you let him blow off steam."

"Your dad never yelled at me." Brooke's chin darted up as she defended her former boss.

Smiling at her loyalty, Atticus stopped. "What I meant was, you were always a calming influence for him."

"I am pretty quiet." Her chin quivered as she tried to hold his gaze, but then it dropped to the middle of his chest.

Well, hell. That wasn't much of a condolence to say to a woman who was more like a kid sister than a coworker. He tucked a finger beneath her chin and nudged it back up, vowing to do better. "After raising four boys who ran roughshod around the house, I think Mom and Dad were both glad you came into their lives." He swiped his thumb over the thick round lenses of her glasses, wiping away the moisture beading there. He wanted her to see the sincerity in his expression. "You were like a daughter to him."

Her eyes were big and slightly almond-shaped. A deeper green than he remembered. They blinked rapidly to erase the sheen of tears gathering there.

Brooke squiggled her chin away from the contact and tugged ever so slightly on his arm to get them walking again. "I'd have done anything for John. He was always good to me."

"He was a good man."

"He was."

They walked the rest of the way without saying a word. Atticus didn't know if he was feeling that same calming influence his dad had always talked about, or if it was just the distance he was putting between himself and Hayley that made the fist squeezing his heart relax its grip. There was a straightforward simplicity to Brooke that was soothing on a day like this.

"Here we are," she announced unnecessarily as they reached the dark-blue compact. She released his arm to dig through her bag for her keys. "You can go now if you want to catch up with your family. Thanks."

"I'll wait until you're inside." Atticus turned in the direction she'd nodded and spotted Sawyer, having a private word with Holden and their mother. With a yes-sir nod to Sawyer, Holden led Susan Kincaid to the black limo she'd ridden in to the service and tucked her inside. Brooke was still rummaging when Atticus turned back to her. He shifted to shield her from the rain with his body and umbrella as the search went into extra innings. "Are you one of those women who carries her life around inside her purse?"

Her chin snapped up and Atticus wondered if it was her natural shyness or just him forcing his company on her that made her so skittish this afternoon. "I like to be prepared."

"For what? The siege of Kansas City?"

Her cheeks flushed and she quickly glanced back down to her purse. She propped one knee up like a stork and rested her bag on her thigh to get to the very bottom. "With my inheritance from my parents, my aunts and I bought a small stone church that we had gutted last fall. Now we're remodeling the inside, shoring up the structure and modernizing the place, putting in central air—we've hired a contractor, of course. But it's only partially finished inside—a bedroom for them, one for me, a bath and part of the kitchen."

When her balance started to waver, Atticus wrapped his hand around her upper arm to steady her. "Easy."

Her foot plopped to the ground and he released her as she kept on talking—using more words than he'd ever heard her string together at any one time. "We barely have closets and we're living out of suitcases because there's still so much dust from the ceiling and drywall work in the main room and the sun porch and deck they're adding on, that I never know when things will be clean or if I can get to them, so I carry... Victory!"

The word *klutzy* had already come to mind by the time she fished out her ring of keys and beamed in triumph. It took another few moments to sort through all of them to find the remote and beep the lock open. There was an endearing absent-minded professor quality to Brooke that was at the far end of the spectrum of chic femininity from a polished professional like Hayley Resnick. Something about her sweet lack of artifice made him want to straighten her glasses on her nose and join the victory celebration with her.

"Allow me." The smile that lightened Atticus's face and mood while he opened the door for her was genuine. With a high-stress job such as his father's, he could definitely see why he'd choose an assistant like Brooke over someone more staid, or perhaps even more experienced. She was uncomplicated. As straightforward and eager to please as she seemed awkward within her own skin. Usually quiet, as she'd said, though he might attribute her bursts of rambling to nervous energy.

And when she smiled as she had a moment ago—over something as inane as finding her keys—the words *plain* and *frumpy* seemed to disappear from Atticus's extensive vocabulary.

"Thank you." She tossed her bag across to the passenger seat where it landed with a thunk. She pushed the door farther open and the rain whipped inside before Atticus could adjust the umbrella. Brooke squinched up her face as the water hit her and she quickly slid behind the wheel and closed the door—leaving a good ten inches of her dark flowered skirt and khaki-green raincoat hanging out and soaking up water from the pavement.

Atticus reached for the door handle at the same time Brooke shoved it open from the inside. The steel door cracked against his knuckles, shooting a tingly flash of pain along every nerve right up his arm. "Damn."

He shook his hand, stirring feeling back into the tips of his fingers.

"I'm sorry."

He flexed his fingers as normal sensation quickly returned. "It's only a minor compound fracture."

"What?"

Her crestfallen look made him feel guilty about the joke. "Relax. It's nothing. I'll live." He opened the door wide and stooped down to rescue the hem of her dress and coat.

She'd turned in her seat, her eyes following his every movement. "I'm sorry."

He wasn't. Sorry, that is. Not with the view he was getting. Right in front of him, stretching out for what seemed like miles and miles, was a smooth, creamy thigh. Long. Shapely. Fit.

When the hell had mousy Brooke sprouted legs like that? Why did she hide them under long skirts and slacks?

And why the hell did he care about unflattering clothes? Or surprisingly flattering appendages?

Rationalizing the instinctive reaction to a pretty stretch of leg as the by-product of the day's stress, Atticus pulled her dress down, covering her up to a more familiar, less distracting level.

"Atticus?" She reached out, her touch so light on his shoulder, he could barely feel the weight of it.

"I'm okay, I promise." He tucked the wet material inside the car and stood, dismissing her touch and her concern. "I'll see you at Mom's."

She nodded, waiting to make sure Atticus stepped safely aside before pulling the door shut. "See you."

He retreated another couple of steps to allow her to pull into the procession of exiting traffic.

Masking his scrutiny with the scalloped point of his umbrella, Atticus scanned the vehicles to make sure Hayley and her male friend had gone. Good. Not a platinum blonde in the bunch. Atticus breathed a heavy sigh, cleansing his conscience. Maybe he should feel bad about using Brooke as an escape from a painful episode from his past. After all, what made his relationship with Hayley so painful was the fact that she had used *him*.

But right now, as he watched the little blue VW zip around a turn and head down the road toward the exit, he was glad he'd chosen to take his walk with Brooke. Not only because she knew more about his father's work than anyone at KCPD, but also because he could use a little peace on a day like today. Might be his only respite for a while. And though Brooke could be a little dangerous to herself and others, she was on the whole, well…peaceful.

Feeling centered enough to get down to the business at hand, Atticus noted the empty copse of trees and set out to join the impromptu Kincaid family reunion.

Chapter Two

"You're no Audrey Hepburn." Brooke Hansford's deadpan critique was as plain and uninspiring as the reflection staring back at her from the plastic-wrapped mirror. So much for the new glasses working miracles.

True, the lenses were narrower and reduced the pop-bottle effect that distorted her nearsighted eyes. And the subtle design of the copper metal frames was more modern and colorful than her last pair had been. She turned her face from side to side, assessing each view.

"Maybe Katharine Hepburn?" Her breath seeped out on a wistful sigh and she reached for her hairbrush. "You wish."

The old movies lied. Switching to contact lenses and trimming three inches off her hair hadn't transformed her from gal Friday to femme fatale. The only male who had gone out of his way to notice her without her glasses was her opthamologist—who'd looked deep into her eyes to study the weeping red irritation of her allergic reaction to the lenses, not because he was entranced by any sudden beauty discovered there.

The UMKC extension class in assertiveness training that she'd taken the past semester had recommended emphasizing her strengths to build confidence when facing a new or difficult situation. Apparently, twenty-twenty vision would never be one of hers. So new glasses it was.

She pulled the brush through the long hair and tamed the bundle into a ponytail. The golden highlights the hairdresser had added were barely noticeable. "Maybe I should go red like Aunt Lou," Brooke speculated, trying to envision how adding an auburn wash to her blond-brown-blah color might somehow help the long curls cooperate with the humidity that was already making the morning air sticky. She should probably take some of the money she was using to make over the small stone church that was now her half-finished home and make herself over. "I wonder what miracles cost these days."

Brooke twisted her hair up and reached for the clip that would anchor it to the back of her head. So much for the boost of confidence the new suit and glasses were supposed to give her as she started work at the Fourth Precinct today. Not that she wasn't excited about the transfer to newly promoted Major Mitch Taylor's office. She was going to be administrative assistant to the man now in charge of every watch and department in the Fourth Precinct offices. She loved the challenges of her career, thrived on making her professional world run efficiently. Working with computers and data, an attention to facts and details—those were definitely strengths of hers where her confidence could truly shine.

Her appearance wasn't the real issue this morning.

The new job wasn't what was making her heart race and her mouth dry.

Even Major Taylor's tough and gruff reputation as a demanding boss didn't really worry her.

It was Atticus Kincaid. *He'd* be there.

Brilliant detective. Tall. Black-haired. Capable of turning her into a stuttering idiot with a direct look or teasing remark. Two weeks of working side by side with him, poring through his late father's files—searching for a lead on John Kincaid's murder and finding nothing useful—had taught her that embarrassing lesson. His broad shoulders and crisp style did wonders for a suit and tie—and frustrated her hormones to no end.

Not one of her smartest moves—developing a crush on a man who looked on her as a kid sister or his father's frumpy secretary. There was a date that was never gonna happen.

Though she and Atticus wouldn't be working in the same office, they'd be working in the same building, possibly on the same floor. No doubt she'd bump into him in the break room, or have to sit across from him at a meeting table.

How was she supposed to be competent and professional around him without getting her crowded thoughts and well-meaning words twisted up inside her throat? Chances were her new coworkers would think she was dimwitted or indifferent or just plain stuck-up before she could help them understand how thrilled and honored she was to be there and be a part of their law-enforcement team.

And the most embarrassing part of it was that Atticus would be patient and polite no matter how badly she and her shy genes fumbled around.

He was as good a son to her former boss, John Kincaid, as all the Kincaid boys had been. And, like the rest of his family, he'd been sweet enough to check on her a couple of times at John's funeral three months ago—even though she'd repaid him with bruised knuckles and mud on his uniform. She had always been so grateful for the Kincaids' kindness to her.

For John Kincaid's sake, she'd bury her misguided attraction and slug her way through her social awkwardness and make a success of herself at the Fourth Precinct.

For John.

Brooke gripped the edge of the sink and held on as a wave of sadness washed over her. Oh, how she missed John and the familiarity of working in his warm, strong presence day in and day out. The grief wasn't with her all the time now, but when she thought about the good friend she had lost—the mentor who had taken her under his wing and shown her what a father was like—the loss caused by his senseless murder made her heartsick all over again.

Yet, almost as quickly as the sadness had hit her, Brooke's frustration with the stalled investigation spurred her out of her funk. She finished pinning up her hair and tucking in her blouse. As the closest thing to an inside man familiar with the comings and goings of John's office, she'd promised the Kincaid family to do whatever she could to help find his killer. Homicide's investigation might have stalled; her research with Atticus might have stalled. But no way was she giving up. Standing in front of the mirror and bemoaning her deficiencies instead of expecting success did John Kincaid's memory a disservice.

Her former boss had seen right through her shy exterior and demanded important things from her. He'd pushed her to use every brain cell, to take chances, to be confident in all she could do. He'd recommended that assertiveness class to her in the first place, said he wanted her to see the same talented woman he saw every day, and to believe in herself. He'd set his expectations for Brooke high, and she'd risen to his challenge.

Now she'd have to do the same for herself. Becoming that self-confident, successful woman John Kincaid believed in would be the best testimonial to the man she could offer.

Any crush she might have on one of his sons—any guilt she might feel at not being able to help him—was irrelevant. She owed this to John.

So, Brooke adjusted the pretty new glasses on her unremarkable face, smoothed her palms down the front of her light-gray gabardine skirt, and silently declared herself ready for the new day ahead. She grabbed her jacket from its garment bag and headed out of the bathroom.

BROOKE HADN'T TAKEN three steps before her good intentions hit their first roadblock.

"Louise! Get down from there." Brooke spotted the artificially strawberry-blond hair nearly two stories above her. She dropped her jacket and ran across the planks of the temporary floor to grab the base of a ladder that soared up to the peak of the nineteenth-century limestone church she and her aunts now called home. "Aunt Lou? We talked about this."

"I'm doing a little patch work on the ceiling."

"On a thirty-foot ladder?"

"How else am I supposed to reach it?" *Smart ass.* Louise Hansford—a ringer for the younger brother who'd been

Brooke's father if the old pictures in her scrapbooks were accurate—pulled a caulking gun from the hammer loop of her denim overalls and squeezed something into a vent where workers were installing a central cooling and heating system. "After all that rain this spring and the leaks we had, I'm not taking any chances on more water damage. We've put too much time and money into the bedrooms and bath downstairs to let problems in the unfinished areas ruin the work we've already done."

"We're paying Mr. McCarthy and his crew good money to do that type of work for us. Now come down." Brooke shifted to the other side of the ladder, hissing through clenched teeth as Louise climbed up to a higher rung to inspect another vent. When nothing fell and no one crashed, Brooke allowed herself a normal breath. "It hasn't rained for two weeks. And unless you count the humidity, there's no moisture in the forecast, either."

"My old bones say different."

"Don't…" *Old bones, my foot.* Brooke got a bug's-eye view of her aunt stepping from the ladder onto the steel scaffolding that gave construction workers access to the aged oak panels lining the arched ceiling. "There's not a thing wrong with your old bones." Louise's occasional bouts with vertigo, however, were another story. "You're sixty-five years old."

"And I'm in better shape than women half my age. Limber, too." She reached through the steel framing and pushed aside the plastic tarp that captured the bulk of the dust and debris from the workmen's sanding and drilling projects.

Oh, no. "Come down and have breakfast," Brooke begged.

But Louise wasn't listening. "Where do you think you get those long limbs of yours from? I'm fine."

Brooke puffed out an irritated sigh—and not just because she was fighting a losing battle with her aunt. Brooke's arms and legs were long and gangly and considerably lacking Louise's spider-like grace. Maybe by the time she turned sixty-five, she might finally manage to outgrow that uncoordinated adolescent phase that was still just as embarrassing now as it had been nine years ago when she'd turned twenty and had no longer qualified as a teenager.

Or maybe she was destined to live out her days dealing with all of the Hansford family's recessive genes. Timidity. Klutziness. Eyes that were too big and boobs that were too small.

Tamping down the inevitable frustration, Brooke moved over to check the anchors on the scaffolding that framed the skeletal stairs and second-floor landing still under construction, fearing there was little more she could do to protect her daredevil of an aunt. "This is why we hired a contractor. If you wait half an hour, Mr. McCarthy and his men will be here to do that job for you."

"I like to keep an eye on their work," Louise insisted. "Some men see three women living together—two of them retired—as an easy mark to take advantage of. That won't happen on my watch. No, sir."

"No one is taking advantage of us." Brooke had studied the numbers meticulously and done her research into the costs of blending modernization with restoration—and who could best do the work for them. Louise was the only thing worrying her right now. Brooke cringed as her aunt tested her weight on one of the two-by-fours that framed the upstairs landing before stepping on it. "Lou?"

But the red-blond hair and overalls had already disappeared through the tarp. Only the creaking of the wooden bracings above her head told her what path Louise was taking to the opposite side of the church. Brooke followed the sounds of her aunt, wondering if she'd be able to catch her should she tumble through one of the open spaces above her.

"I know as much about building and restoring things as any man." Louise was a disembodied voice from the rafters overhead. "I've got a degree in architectural history, don't I? Truman McCarthy doesn't have one of those."

So that's what had spurred this show of independence. It wasn't really concern that the work wasn't being done properly, but a regret that once upon a time, Louise Hansford would have been doing the work herself.

Brooke's heart went out to the woman who'd curtailed her globetrotting adventures the day she'd received a telegram telling her of the car crash in Sarajevo that had orphaned Brooke, and had come home to help her older sister, Peggy, take care of their parentless niece. Once a woman ahead of her time, Louise's life had become considerably more mundane, serving first as surrogate parent and in more recent years as best friend. In time, as her aunts aged, their roles would reverse, and Brooke would gladly step up to take care of the two women who were the only family she'd ever known. That was one of the reasons she was creating this spacious home, so that her aunts could live independently on the main floor, while Brooke eventually moved upstairs to a private apartment.

But the future would have to wait until she could get Louise down to a safer altitude. Hurrying back to the base of the ladder, Brooke hiked her skirt up above her knees.

"I know you're an expert." She toed off her pumps and climbed the first rung. "But McCarthy and Sons is a reputable company. They don't do shoddy work."

"Now don't you go climbin' up there after her," Peggy Hansford chided as she stepped out into the main room and closed the bedroom door behind her. The elder Hansford aunt picked up Brooke's jacket from the floor and brushed it off. She motioned Brooke down as she strode past the ladder into the nearly finished kitchen area. "No sense both of you breakin' your fool necks."

"I can hear you up here, Peggy," Louise hollered.

"Didn't say anything was wrong with your ears. Just your common sense." Peggy draped the jacket over the back of one of the stools they were using for temporary kitchen furniture and turned to pull three mugs out of the dishwasher. "Now you come on down from there. You're worrying Brooke, and we don't want anything to upset her this morning."

Brooke returned to the floor and smoothed her skirt back into place, slipping into her shoes while she waited for Louise to join them. Listening to the woman-sized cat scrambling overhead, she nibbled anxiously on her bottom lip.

But Louise didn't have any speeds except go and go faster, and she quickly popped through the tarp and headed for the ladder. "That's right. You start your new job downtown today." Brooke had barely shrugged into her jacket when Louise pulled up a stool beside her at the black granite counter. "Is that what you're wearing?"

"Louise Hansford." Peggy pointed a reprimanding finger from the opposite side of the island counter.

"Well, she's not even thirty years old yet, and she dresses more conservatively than either one of us."

"She's dressed professionally, Lou." Peggy's soft green eyes expressed a clear opinion over the rims of her glasses. "Besides, I don't think a woman wearing a tie-dye T-shirt and overalls has the right to criticize anyone's wardrobe."

"At least my clothes have personality." Louise plucked at the starched white collar of Brooke's short-sleeved blouse. "Maybe just a scarf to soften things up? Or some funky jewelry to add a little pizzazz?"

"I'm wearing the gold chain you gave me for my twenty-first birthday." Brooke pulled the necklace from her cleavage and held up the nickel-sized charm that had been left to her by her father. "You said Dad asked the nurses to pin this to my diaper in the hospital before he died. I thought it'd be good luck to wear a family heirloom today."

"It *is* good luck. And very pretty, dear." Peggy pushed the French vanilla creamer across the counter to flavor their coffee. "I wish you could have known Leo. I can't tell you how many times he wrote me about you—even before you were born. Your daddy thought you were the most beautiful baby in the world. As beautiful as your mother, God rest her soul."

Aunt Peggy was being too kind. According to the one family photo that had survived the automobile crash which had killed her mother outright and put her father in the hospital for the last few days of his life, Irina Zorinsky Hansford had been a Slavic beauty with curling mahogany tresses and bold, dark eyes. Brooke, only six months old at the time, had survived the fiery accident, miraculously unscathed. She would have ended up in a state-run orphanage if these two strong women hadn't come into her life.

She'd heard the story dozens of times growing up.

Her father had been feverish with burns and grief, too weak to even make arrangements for his wife's hasty funeral, much less attend. But he'd been clear about one thing. *Don't let Brooke go with her mother,* Leo Hansford had pleaded from his hospital bed. *Don't let my baby girl die.*

Brooke and her aunts had never even seen Irina's grave. It had been hard enough proving guardianship and getting out of the country where her father had worked at the American embassy. As soon as they were able, Peggy and Louise had whisked her back to the United States. They'd promised their brother they'd take her home to Kansas City where they'd grown up. Leo Hansford had wanted Brooke to live. Love. Be loved.

She *was* loved.

But she was a pale shadow of the woman her mother had been.

"Well, of course, *we* know what a beautiful girl she is." Louise hugged Brooke around the shoulders, breaking the pensive mood. "But how is anyone else going to notice when she dresses like a nun?" Louise snapped her fingers, already turning for the bedroom she shared with Peggy as an idea hit her. "I'll be right back. I have a brooch in my suitcase that will add a shot of color and liven things up a bit."

Peggy tied an apron around her plump middle, shaking her head. "You know, sometimes I think we're raising her more than she and I ever had to raise you. Thank God you have your father's steady nature and good sense. And tact!" she shouted after her sister.

Brooke tucked the medallion with the Cyrillic letter etched in gold back inside her blouse. As much as *steady nature* and *good sense* felt like faint praise, she had to grin at Peggy's on-the-money assessment of their family dynamic.

"You know, we'll have to nail her shoes to the floor when we start painting the bedrooms. The fumes will go straight to her head and make her dizzy. Dizzi*er*," Brooke amended, eliciting a smile and reassuring Peggy that Louise's remarks had no lasting effect on her ego. Brooke sipped her coffee and reached for one of the English muffins Peggy was toasting for breakfast. "I told her that I was going to hire someone specifically to do odd jobs like that around here. At lunch today I'm interviewing a man Mr. McCarthy recommended." She thumbed over her shoulder toward the ceiling. "When we agreed to cut a few costs by completing the finish and landscaping work ourselves, I didn't mean having either one of you hanging from the scaffolding or doing some other dangerous thing."

"I'm already ahead of you, dear." Peggy winked and dropped her voice to a conspiratorial whisper. "I've let the weeds grow in my garden and we'll have to turn up the soil before anyone can lay new sod, so I've got plenty lined up for her to do outside while you're painting."

Brooke winked back and reached across the island to squeeze Peggy's hand. "You're the real smart cookie of the bunch, aren't you?"

Peggy turned her hand and squeezed back. "You can have Lou's long arms and legs. My brains will get you further any day of the week."

"I found it." Louise beamed with the satisfaction of a fairy godmother admiring her magical handiwork when she returned. Urging Brooke to stand, she pinned a silver brooch with a lapis, turquoise and coral mosaic onto her lapel. "I got this on a trip to New Mexico when I was in college. A young gentleman classmate insisted I have it. There. That brightens things up. Smile for me." As generous as she was honest, Louise cupped Brooke's cheek and smiled back. "Now *that*, my dear, is your most beautiful asset."

"Thanks."

Lou twirled her finger into a tendril that curled over Brooke's cheek and tucked it behind her ear. "Have you thought about one of those short, kicky hairstyles? Maybe some golden highlights?"

"You can't tell I put in highlights?"

"Leave her alone," Peggy reproved. "Brooke looks just fine."

"*Fine,* sure." Lou climbed onto the stool beside Brooke and doctored her coffee with a spoonful of sugar. "But what about sexy? Or hot? I mean, I was never drop-dead gorgeous, but I always knew how to work what I have."

"Enough." Blushing around her last bite of muffin, Brooke stood and checked her watch. Though she was in no danger of being late, she could only handle so much of her aunt playing Cinderella with Brooke in the title role. "Even if you dolled me up, I could never pull off *hot*. Besides, I'm going to work, not to some fancy ball to pick up a man."

Lou cradled her mug between her hands, shaking her head. "All those men in uniforms and badges and she's not trying to pick one up."

"Lou…" Peggy warned. "Don't put that kind of pressure on her. Brooke is just a late bloomer. When the right man comes along, he'll see her real beauty."

"Yes, but you know how dense men can be. It doesn't hurt to help them find their way."

Brooke's blush heated her clear down to her toes now. Louise didn't have a shy bone in her body—she'd never understood how it made Brooke's perfectly intelligent brain seize up whenever she tried to break out of her shell and try to get a man she was attracted to to notice her.

Buying herself some time to gather her thoughts and slip her newly forged assertive armor back into place, Brooke picked up her purse from the card table that served as living-room furniture, and dug out a tube of copper-colored lip gloss. Only after she'd put her professional game face back in place did she loop her carryall bag over her shoulder and turn to Louise. "Tell you what. I'll make a deal with you." She pointed across the main room. "You stay off that ladder and I'll make the effort to talk to… three…men today."

"About something *not* work-related," Lou qualified, setting down her mug and smiling with hope.

"Agreed."

"Then you've got a deal."

"You're a hopeless romantic, Lou. But I love ya." Brooke squeezed her aunt in a hug. She traded another hug with Peggy at the back door. "Love you, too."

"Don't worry. I'll keep her out of trouble. You just concentrate on the new job and have a wonderful first day."

"I will. See you tonight."

Brooke crossed the sundeck that had yet to have a railing added, and bopped down the stairs at the opposite end. The sun was warm on her face as she crossed the yard to where her car was parked at the curb. The tall, broken grass packed into the dry dirt where Truman McCarthy and his construction crew drove their heavy equipment and supply trucks up to the house reminded her to start pricing carports. When winter hit, it'd be a bear to have to trek through the snow or shovel a path out to the street. And the historical value of the church's turn-of-the-century exterior wouldn't allow her to attach a modern garage.

But the remodeling notes were only a minor diversion from the real concern at hand as Brooke dug her keys from her purse. She'd made a promise to her aunt. Now she had to keep it. Talk to a man. Pick one up, if Louise had her way. It could happen. Right. Brooke nearly snorted, squelching her ironic laughter.

Think positive. Be positive. The new and slowly improving Brooke could do this. She just needed to break the task down into smaller, less-daunting goals, and not psych herself out over the bigger challenge of transforming into the social butterfly Aunt Lou believed she could be.

Three men. She could do that. "Hi" qualified as speaking to a man, didn't it? "I'm Major Taylor's new administrative assistant" could be an entire conversation at a busy office.

Sure, she'd love to have a man notice her for something more than her computer skills, to have him think she was something special. But she'd pick smaller battles, savor lesser victories, instead of setting herself up for failure. She wasn't going to let Louise's fairy-godmother fantasies make or break her day. Or her life.

She'd have plenty of interesting things to do at the Fourth Precinct, meeting coworkers and learning new routines. Plus, there was the work here at home. She had love in her life from her aunts and friends. She didn't need Prince Charming to make her happy or make her feel complete.

Still, it wouldn't hurt a girl's ego to…

A subtle, external awareness seeped into Brooke's thoughts, short-circuiting the endless debate. The sun was already bright in the cloudless sky, yet a chill slunk down her spine and she halted beside her car.

She slowly turned, seeking the source.

It was that same odd sensation she got watching a DVD by herself late at night, when she was reminded of how Alfred Hitchcock's suspenseful timing combined with her ever-churning imagination could totally spook her. Only this wasn't something she could turn off with the remote.

She zeroed in on a dented tan pickup truck parked a block down the street. Brooke adjusted her glasses at the temple and squinted.

Who was that? She didn't recognize the vehicle or its occupant behind the steering wheel, though she could make out little more than the man's snow-white hair. But he wasn't old, not if the ripples of muscle beneath his T-shirt were any indication. He was almost faceless with his head hunched down into his shoulders and his purple K-State ball cap pulled low over his eyes. Was he lost? Sleeping?

Watching her?

He shifted in his seat and Brooke quickly turned away, avoiding any possibility of eye contact by staring down at her fingers on the door handle. "Paranoid much?"

Her nerves about starting the new job had gotten the better of her common sense, that was all. This was a regular old Monday morning in the middle of July, not a Hitchcock movie. And the Wildcat fan was nothing more than a man in a truck.

Brooke lifted her chin, determined to dispel her suspicion. She saw her aunts through the tall, narrow church windows, moving inside the house. There was a trio of boys two houses down, marking the bases for an early-morning whiffle ball game. Farther down the street, she spotted another neighbor, Mrs. Boyer, hanging on to the leash of her Labradoodle puppy as they practiced their daily walk.

All normal. All familiar.

Except…

Him.

"Stop it." Brooke yanked open the car door and tossed her bag across the seat before she was tempted to look his way again. The man was probably one of Truman McCarthy's construction workers, who'd shown up early for his shift and was waiting for his foreman to arrive. She was the only one who spent so much time with the thoughts inside her head that she could turn a harmless observation into a threat. No one else in the neighborhood seemed to think anything was out of place. Why should she?

Dismissing the man, the truck and the creepy sixth sense her imagination had concocted, Brooke hiked her skirt a notch and climbed inside to start the car and drive away.

But only a few minutes later, she began to wonder if her imagination had been playing tricks on her, after all. Stopped at a light before turning onto the highway which would take her into downtown Kansas City, Brooke checked her rearview mirror. Her breath hitched and she looked again.

Three vehicles behind her. Waiting to turn onto the same highway.

The stranger in the dented tan pickup truck.

Chapter Three

"I'm familiar with the program, sir." Brooke hugged two software documentation manuals to her chest, wondering if Mitch Taylor had any idea how much space his broad shoulders and thick, barrel chest took up in her small, freshly painted but otherwise undecorated outer office. "But it'll certainly be helpful to go through the formal training tomorrow."

"Good." His deep, commanding voice seemed to bounce off the safety glass on the door between their offices. "I'm competent when it comes to computers, but I'll be counting on you to understand all the tricky stuff."

"Yes, sir."

"And unless it's the commissioner, my wife or one of my sons or daughter calling, I don't want to talk to anyone before the morning briefing."

"Won't the watch commanders handle the briefing of each shift?"

"They'll handle the briefing. But they'll meet with me first."

"Yes, sir." Brooke jotted the note on the pad at her desk.

Watch commander meeting—no calls but the ones that count. She set down her pen and looked up. "Any other daily routine items I should know, Major Taylor?"

"Today, just handle the phone. Get your feet under you, unpack these boxes, and we'll figure out the rest as we go along this week."

"Yes, sir."

A smile softened the rugged line of his jaw. "It's Mitch. You don't have to use the *Mister* or *Major* or *sir* when it's just us talking." He extended his long arm across her desk. "Welcome to the Fourth, Brooke."

She reached out to shake his hand, "Thank you, sir—" Her shaky smile relaxed into the real deal. "Thanks, Mitch."

"That's better." He seemed to approve of her effort to blur the line between efficiency and informality. Pulling back the front of his jacket, he propped his hands at his waist, subconsciously emphasizing the badge clipped to his belt, and giving her a glimpse of the gun and holster he wore beneath his right arm. Mitch Taylor was clearly a man who led men, but he seemed to have a little more teddy bear in him than his grizzly reputation had led her to believe. He surveyed her office, stopping when he spotted the plants she'd set on one of the empty bookshelves. "I see you have a fan club."

Way to impress the boss, Hansford. He'd left flowers on her desk for when she arrived that morning, and she hadn't said boo about them. Brooke set the stack of manuals on the corner of her desk and crossed to the shelf, fingering the delicate white petals and reading the attached card that welcomed her and wished her luck.

"Thank you for the daisies. They're…" *A lovely gesture.*

A bright addition to the office. One of my favorite flowers.
"They're nice."

Nice? With her back to her boss, Brooke rolled her eyes.
A dozen eloquent thank-yous had run through her head,
and all that came out of her mouth was *They're nice?* No
wonder Louise worried about her ability to carry on a
personal conversation with a man.

"Glad you like them. Though, I will confess, my wife,
Casey, thought of them."

"She has good taste," Brooke stumbled on, fighting to
get her thoughts ahead of her words. She turned to face
him. "Tell her thank you, too."

"I will." Including his wife seemed to please him, which
pleased Brooke. "We'd better get to work then, hadn't we?"

"Yes, sir." He held up a cautionary finger, and Brooke
almost laughed. "Right, Mitch," she corrected herself.

With a wink, he opened the adjoining door between
their offices and left her to get acquainted with bookshelves
and file drawers, a state-of-the-art computer system and
boxes of supplies that needed to find a home.

That was *one*. Louise better not be climbing that ladder.
Brooke had only two more conversations to go.

Standing a little straighter and smiling more easily,
Brooke opened the blinds covering the windows of her
outer office, spying on the stream of uniformed and plain-
clothes officers outside. The shift must be changing for
there to be so much traffic leading from the bank of elevators to the sergeant's desk and main room beyond. From
her hallway, cubicle walls blocked her view of the detectives' desks and interview rooms. And she already knew the
conference and break rooms were around the corner down

another hall. Mitch Taylor's quick tour this morning had already familiarized her with the layout of the Fourth's headquarters building, if not with all the people on the other side of that glass.

Turning away before her confidence wavered, Brooke took off her jacket and hung it on the back of her chair. She resumed organizing file cabinets and her desk in a way that would be most efficient for her. After depositing an armload of paper onto the bottom bookshelf, she paused to stretch and admire her flowers.

She didn't get gifts delivered to her very often, but this morning she had three plants to brighten her office—the daisies from Major Taylor and his wife, a pot of draping English ivy from her aunts and a pink carnation with a hand-scrawled note from the pseudo big brother she *didn't* have a crush on, Sawyer Kincaid. *Do great, kiddo! You'll rock the Fourth. Love ya, Sawyer.*

"I love ya, too, big guy." Atticus's older brother Sawyer was easy to like, easy to talk to—maybe because he was so crazy in love with his new wife and stepson that Brooke knew there'd never be another woman in his life, so she never felt any pressure to fill any other role besides sister. Equally likely was that Sawyer, unlike his enigmatic brother, was always out there with his emotions. He spoke what he thought—whether he was angry or being goofy or falling in love. There were no secrets or second-guessing with him.

"Ah." *Revelation.* Maybe it was her love for puzzles and the challenge of solving mysteries that fueled her crush on Atticus Kincaid.

And maybe it was the safety of knowing *he* was a mystery she was never going to crack that only made her think she had a thing for him. If he was unattainable, she could pine away without ever having to put her fragile sense of self out there.

And she'd called Aunt Louise a hopeless romantic.

"Too much thinking," Brooke chided. Her overly analytical brain was great for computers, but it could wreak havoc on a gal's love life.

Knowing that focusing on something outside herself was the best way to curtail the sabotaging train of thought, she picked up Sawyer's gift and moved the bloom to her desk where she could enjoy it as she dove back into her work. The number of times she answered the phone and transferred or took messages over the next two hours gave her a pretty good idea of just how busy she was going to be in this new position—and how much she was going to love it.

Brooke was more than ready to take a break at eleven-thirty. She pulled a bottle of water from her bag, kicked off her pumps beneath her desk and sat back to wiggle her toes and admire her handiwork. The layout of her computer and desktop now made the best use of light and workspace. Her shelves were pleasingly arranged and gave her easy access to the items she'd need most. And her chin-high file cabinets had been alphabetized and organized within an inch of their lives.

Really, all that was left were the personal touches that would make the new surroundings feel like her own place. The flowers helped for now, but she'd bring a couple of reading books to keep on the shelves for her lunch break, maybe frame some of the photographs of the reconstruction project at home and hang them on the wall above the file cabinets.

"Ooh, my pictures." The thought reminded her of the photos of Peggy and Lou that she liked to keep on her desk. Spinning her chair around, she picked up the box from beside the desk and pulled it up onto her lap. Smiling as she removed the lid and fingered through the precious items inside, Brooke sorted through sentimental knick-knacks, framed certificates and diplomas and pulled out the two photographs. "There you are, ladies."

Brooke propped the box on the corner of the desk as she stood, arranging the pictures at the top of her desk calendar blotter. Reenergized by the familiar memories, she continued to unpack and decorate, padding around the office in her stocking feet, finding just the right spot for everything.

But as she reached into the bottom of the box, her heart seized up. "Oh, John," she whispered reverently. "You found it."

She sank into her chair as she pulled out the worn leather journal where she'd kept a log about the highs and lows of her life at work. She had several similar journals locked up in a trunk at home. She'd kept many such books in the years of her life since adolescence, when a visit to the counselor over her near inability to talk at school—and the resulting ulcers and hives that were sure indicators of stress— had led to the advice that she express her thoughts and emotions in whatever way she could. She'd punched pillows and squeezed worry dolls. Shouted and cussed in the privacy of her aunts' basement. And if she was too shy to talk, she could write things down—her dreams, her fears, her anger and compassion, who she liked at school, why her aunts were being too strict, what she and her friends had done together that was particularly exciting and more. The adolescent therapy had evolved into a personal history of sorts over the years.

This particular journal, in which she'd first conceived the idea of finding an historic structure in a quiet suburb to remake into the perfect blend of rich character and modern amenities, had gone missing a couple of months before her boss's death. For a few awful days, Brooke thought she'd sent it out with a package of evidence reports to the state lab. She'd turned her desk and purse and file cabinets inside out, searching for the lost journal, and had even called a friend in the KCPD archives, asking her to check through the boxed-up files that had been shipped from the deputy commissioner's office. In the end, Brooke had accepted that she'd set the book down at a lunch table or park bench and had walked away without it. It would have been thrown out by the time she went back to look for it.

But John had found it, bless his heart. A sticky note on the front read *For Brooke* in his slanted, distinctive scrawl. Even after he was gone, he was, "Still looking out for me, aren't you?"

Brooke opened the book and found a second sticky note inside the front cover. *Forgive me* this one said. "For what?" she mused, frowning. She'd forgive him anything. "Did you stick this in your briefcase by mistake? Read a couple of pages?" She talked to the book as though the man who'd snuck it back into her personal belongings could hear her. "Trust me. The content of this book is tame compared to what I've got at home." No mention of how good-looking his sons were, or how grateful she was to be accepted as part of his family. Just business stuff. Just things she didn't mind sharing at work. She hoped.

Oh, Lordy. What if some of those really personal things *had* found their way in here? Like a page of curse words over a particularly frustrating day, or something equally embarrassing?

Thumbing through the pages, Brooke figuratively held her breath and reminisced. There was the day she'd first started in John's office, replacing his retiring assistant. She'd been so nervous. John had seemed so commanding, so busy that morning. She half suspected he hadn't even noticed that she'd arrived. He'd been in the middle of a task force investigation and something on the case had broken. After he'd snapped an order for her to get online and find out everything she could about Wolfe International's accounts in London and the Cayman Islands, Brooke had slid behind her desk and gone right to work with little more than an exchange of names. He'd seemed pleased— even impressed—when she set the printouts on his table in the briefing room that afternoon. He'd called her into the office at the end of the day, apologized and informed her that he'd be taking her to breakfast the next morning—if she could stand to spend time with an old grouch like him.

Brooke rolled her eyes at the smiley face she'd drawn at the end of that entry. "I decided I liked you, after all."

When she turned the page to read how much more smoothly day two had gone, Brooke gasped. There, in the margin, next to her own neat writing was a scrawled comment from John.

"I knew I liked you that first day, too," it read.

He *had* read the journal. "Oh, please don't tell me I wrote anything stupid in this one."

Sitting up straight, Brooke read through the journal

page by page. She found another comment about how it creeped him out at first to have this quiet stranger predict his needs—sometimes before he knew them—as well as keep him on schedule. Brooke smiled when she found the note about how crazy he thought she was to buy the old stone church. "Waste of an inheritance," it said. "Too big a money pit for a sweet thing like you." Then, a page later, he wrote a lengthy missive about his fascination with the history of the church after she'd given him a tour and described her plans for the conversion. He'd gotten caught up in the building's history and how it related to the settlement of the city and how he'd love to tackle a similar restoration project when he retired. He was impressed with Brooke's businesslike approach and her determination to maintain the integrity of the historic design when it came to the remodel. He called her a "damn lucky girl to be able to pursue a dream like that."

Tears, both told-you-so happy and I-miss-you-so regret, filled her eyes and blurred her vision until she had to reach up beneath her glasses and wipe them away. She turned the page to discover a boxy sketch with letters that didn't form words, and symbols that made no sense.

"This isn't mine." She shook her head at the curious creative expression John had drawn in her journal. "And you said *I* was crazy."

The phone rang, startling Brooke from the trip down memory lane. The journal fell to the floor when she jumped. "Good grief." Pressing a hand to her racing heart, she took a deep breath and picked up the receiver and her pen. "KCPD, Fourth Precinct, this is Major Taylor's office."

"Miss Hansford?"

"Yes?"

"This is the front desk downstairs. There's a Tony Fierro here to see you. He says you're expecting him?"

"Oh. Um…" The job interview for the handyman. Was there a problem? "Do I need to go down there to see him, or can he come upstairs?"

"It's up to you, ma'am. I can give him a visitor's pass."

Just a security protocol. Nothing to worry about. She needed to end her trip down memory lane and start looking to the future again. "Then, as soon as he clears security, go ahead and send him up, please."

"Will do, ma'am."

Once the call ended, Brooke squatted to get her shoes. But her sleeve caught the corner of the box and pulled it down to the floor beside her, spilling its contents. "Attack of the Killer Klutz strikes again," she muttered, shifting onto her hands and knees to right the box and retrieve papers, books and some wayward pencils. Her necklace and charm swung out like a pendulum from the front of her blouse, and she paused to catch it and tuck it back in. In the midst of crawling and tucking, something caught her eye. She squeezed the charm in her fist as she studied the image beneath her. "Is that my house?"

Hovering over the open pages, Brooke peered down at the now-sideways drawing. "What were you up to, John?"

There were dots and arrows and scribbled phrases marking the picture. Apparently, he'd thought he had a better plan as to how she should redesign the stone church's interior. From this angle, what she'd excused as a meaningless doodle now looked like a crude architectural drawing.

No. Like a map.

But to what?

Brooke's heart beat a little faster and new brain cells awoke.

"That *is* my house." She traced the lines with her fingertip, identifying the original altar area of the church that had since been lined with windows and converted into a sun porch. "Three," she read aloud. Had he wanted to add more rooms? "It's a supporting exterior wall, John. You can't budge rock like that. Three plug-ins? Three windows? Three…what?" More scribbles took shape. "B6N-NR." An arrow pointed to an archway.

"B. 6. N. Basement? Brick? Board? North…Room?" Brooke squinted and rotated the drawing, as though better vision or a different angle would help the jumbled characters make sense. "There is no north room."

No basement, either. Just a crawl space.

"Lose something?"

A deep, familiar voice, laced with amusement, greeted her from the doorway.

Atticus.

Brooke snapped the journal shut and jerked her head up. He leaned against the door frame, one hand behind his back, looking as perfectly at home in that tailored suit as he did wearing the gun and badge at his belt.

Meanwhile, she was shoeless, scattered and practically sprawled on the floor.

Every self-conscious cell in her body flooded her brain, blocking rational thought as words automatically popped out. "Mitch isn't here. He's gone to lunch."

He chuckled, low in his throat. "Hi to you, too. I stopped by to see how you were settling in."

The masculine pitch of his laughter danced across her eardrums and did funny things to her pulse rate, tying up her thoughts into even more of a knot.

"Sorry. Hi. Fine." *Brilliant conversation, Sherlock.* Ah, yes, this was that moment of babbling stupidity that had plagued her nerves this morning. Aunt Lou had been right to worry. Breathing deeply, Brooke clutched the journal to her chest and ducked her head, buying herself a few moments to reassert control over her instinctive reactions by collecting a handful of pencils and dropping them into the box.

Black oxford shoes and charcoal slacks crossed the room until the gun and badge filled her peripheral vision. "Need some help?"

"I can get it." But it had been a rhetorical question. She heard a clunk on her desktop just before miles of wide shoulders and charcoal jacket descended to her level.

Despite her insistence, Atticus knelt beside her to help pick up her mess. He wasn't a man who wore cologne, but there was a clean maleness clinging to his clothes that made her want to turn her cheek into his starchy white shirt and silk tie. Maybe she'd unbutton that shirt to see if the warm skin underneath smelled even better.

Alarmed at the boldness of her thoughts, Brooke scooted after a folder of motivational quotes from her assertiveness class and straightened the scattered pages. She stole a glance at Atticus's sharp jaw and gunmetal eyes, double-checking to see that she hadn't revealed anything more embarrassing than her lack of coordination. Being attracted to the man was one thing—being attracted to the man and having him *know* she had these crazy impulses when she was around him was something else entirely.

No-nonsense hands that were strong and agile quickly scooped up the last of the items and lifted the box onto her desk. She stared at one of those hands as it reached out to help her up. Brooke lightly touched her fingers to his, but he wrapped his palm around hers for a firmer grip and pulled her to her feet. "Up you go."

As practical and impersonal as the helping hand had been, Brooke was still feeling flushed with heat as she stood and spotted the clear vase filled with a half-dozen red roses sitting on the far corner of her desk.

"You brought me flowers" came out before "Thank you." She reached out to stroke the velvety soft petals. When had any man given her such a gorgeous, dramatic arrangement?

Her incredulity was short-lived. Atticus tucked his hands casually into the pockets of his slacks and shrugged. "Sorry, they're not from me."

She curled her fingers into her palm and tried not to feel disappointed. "Oh."

Brooke searched for a tag while he explained. "I'm just the deliveryman. I've been meaning to drop by all morning but I had to make an appearance in court, and then I had some calls to follow up on with a case and, well, the sarge caught me walking past her desk and handed them off. Gave me a good excuse to stop what I was doing and come see you."

He'd waited until someone asked him to stop by? The nick at her ego was eased by the knowledge that he didn't seem at all aware of the awkward affection she felt for him.

Before embarrassing herself any further, Brooke turned her attention back to the anonymous bouquet. Sergeant Maggie Wheeler had been the first officer to greet Brooke that morning and introduce herself. Though tall and imposing, she'd been friendly enough. Was this another welcome-to-the-precinct gift? "Did Sergeant Wheeler say who they were from?"

"No. She just apologized for being too busy to get them to you sooner." He must have recognized the increasing consternation of her search for a nonexistent card. "Sarge told me the delivery guy said you'd know who they were from."

Brooke frowned. "Really?"

"Got a secret admirer I don't know about?"

Did she? Brooke's single chuckle lacked humor. Sparing him a quick glance that didn't quite meet his gaze, she turned the vase from side to side and worked her bottom lip between her tongue and teeth. Thoughts of the tan pickup that had followed her all the way downtown, never leaving her rearview mirror until she'd turned into the Fourth Precinct parking lot and he drove on past, came to mind. Were the roses another unexplained coincidence? She liked a good mystery, but she preferred to read them rather than be caught up in the middle of one herself.

"Brooke?" She jerked at the warm touch on her elbow. Atticus pulled back, holding up both hands in apology. "You okay?"

"Sure. I'm fine. Just a little perplexed." She turned the vase back to its original position, then picked it up and moved it to the bookshelves behind her, as the bloodred blooms bothered her more than they pleased her. "It's not like I get flowers every day, so I'm just trying to sort things out in my head. I can't think of who would send them. Probably the deputy commissioner's office wishing me luck on the new job. That must be it. I'll have to call the florist and ask."

"Are you sure you're all right? You're talking ninety miles a minute."

"Am I? Well, that's a switch from the girl who won't open her mouth to say anything."

His eyes narrowed and she felt his scrutiny as clearly as she'd felt the brush of his hand. "I know you're a little shy. But if you're trying to say something to me, say it. I'll listen."

He would? Brooke inhaled a deep breath. She could try. *Don't wimp out.* This could be conversation number two. No, this could be something much more important. Atticus was a trained investigator. His job was to piece together clues. Forget the roses. Forget the truck. Forget her timidity. "May I show you something?"

She nearly sent the box flying again when she pulled out the journal and turned to face him. He caught the box and pushed it to a safer location at the middle of her desk, grinning as he answered. "You can try."

"I think I just found a message from your father."

Chapter Four

"A message from Dad?" Atticus's mouth tightened into a grim line, controlling any outward expression of the pain that stabbed through him at the mention of his late father. "What do you mean?"

She laid a brown leather book in his hands and pointed to the sticky note on the cover, penned in John Kincaid's distinctive handwriting. *For Brooke.* "Take a look inside."

"This was Dad's?"

"Mine, actually. I thought I'd lost it. But I guess John found it. He made several entries—some are comments for me, but others don't make sense. I just unpacked it this morning." She hugged her arms across her stomach and raised an expectant gaze over the rims of her glasses. "Maybe I'm being hopeful and reading more into it than what's there. But it's as if your dad was trying to tell me something, but in secret, so I wouldn't find it right away. Almost…" A despairing sigh eased from her chest. "Almost as though he knew something was going to happen to him, and he was leaving bits of advice and making a record of—"

her verdant gaze fell to the book and she hugged herself a little more tightly "—of I don't know what."

Atticus pulled his reading glasses out of his pocket and began to skim. Pain receded into curiosity, and curiosity tapped into something harder at the core of him. He'd always been driven to find the truth. The truth about his father's murder, in particular, wouldn't let him rest until he had answers. "Forgive him for what? Reading your diary?"

"I think it's more than that." The tip of that pink tongue snuck out to worry her bottom lip again.

Stop noticing things like that.

Rechanneling his powers of observation, Atticus propped his hip on the corner of her desk and kept reading. Unlike Brooke, he refused to hope that this was any kind of break in a case that had stalled to the point of growing cold. But if there was anything that might even remotely point them in the direction of his father's killer, or the reason why some bastard thought his father had to die, he intended to find it.

He could tell something had upset Brooke. At first he'd thought it was just embarrassment that he'd caught her wiggling her sweet little backside at him while she crawled across the floor—and for a split second he worried that she'd caught a glimpse of his unwitting admiration before he covered his surprise with an amused grin.

He was relieved when she turned to face him and he could see she was the same old Brooke. Well, not exactly the same. She wore new specs that enhanced the blushing undertones of her pale complexion. And though her hair was in its practical bun, there was something softer about the face, something richer in the caramel color.

But the fact there was a mess, and Brooke was in the middle of it, reassured him that this was the same girl who'd become a part of his family when she'd started to work for his father five years ago.

"I hope there isn't anything too personal in this one," Brooke added. *This* one? There were more journals? More information he could sort through?

Shortly after the funeral, they'd spent two weeks going through anything of his dad's that Kevin Grove and his homicide team hadn't bundled up for evidence. They'd found nothing. Frustrated beyond imagining and feeling as if he'd failed his father, Atticus had dived into his work at the precinct. But he'd never stopped poking around where he could, analyzing anything, no matter how insignificant, that might lead him to the truth. Was Brooke's journal a fresh lead? Or just a sentimental journey that would cause him fresh pain?

As he read through each comment his father had written, Atticus became aware of Brooke bouncing her toe on the gray carpet. Brooke showing impatience? Somehow he'd imagined gentle, sweet and quiet was the extent of her personality. He ignored the toe-tapping and read on.

But then, with a little huff of air, Brooke reached out and flipped the book to a page near the back. "What do you make of that? John sketched it after my last entry."

Atticus assessed the rough dimensions of the lines and arrows. "Why would Dad draw a blueprint of your house?"

Brooke's face lit up. "That's what I thought it was, too. At first I thought he was a wannabe architect, or that he wanted to give me some tips for the safest, roomiest house

I could get—he seemed to think I needed to be taken care of. But if that's the case, then why write his notes in code?" She pointed to the numbers and symbols. "I don't know what any of this other stuff means. Do you?"

"Not off the top of my head." Atticus put away his black-framed glasses and looked into her upturned face. "These abbreviations remind me of text messaging. Is that something you two shared at work?"

"Your dad and technology?" Was that a scoff? "I don't think so. I learned to decipher some pretty sketchy short-hand over the years. But nothing standard. And these are so out of context I don't know what to make of them. Yet. I want to think about it a bit. It's been long enough since I've worked on his papers that I'm out of practice."

"Long enough? Hell." The stab of emotion caught him off guard. His dad had only been gone three months. Though his brain understood what Brooke meant, his heart felt the distance between him and his father growing more each minute.

"I didn't mean—"

"I know you didn't." Her pale, apologetic face swam before his eyes, and Atticus had to move away to recover his emotional balance. He straightened and paced to Major Taylor's door, dredging up a memory from nearly a year ago, though it seemed like only yesterday that he'd sat down with his dad in an office not unlike this one.

Even as a grown man, Atticus had turned to his father for advice. That evening he'd been worried that his career as a cop was going to end up in the toilet after his name and face—and a key witness—had been splashed all over the news before KCPD had planned to release the information. He'd been seeing Hayley Resnick at the time, and believed the ground rules regarding their professional lives had been clear. Sure, he'd fed her some tips when he could; she'd done the same for him. But what he'd regarded as an off-the-record conversation had turned into front-page news, jeopardizing an investigation, endangering the witness and destroying his trust.

Hayley got a promotion for breaking the story and, having tapped out his usefulness to her, moved out of his life. Meanwhile, Atticus got stuck with a ring, a reprimand and egg on his face. John Kincaid had put it all into perspective for his son. *You're a good cop. About the sharpest one I know. Your pride is what took the biggest hit here. The jokes and gossip will stop once you remind everyone what you can do. A mistake like this won't kill your career. But it can kill your ability to love another woman. Don't let that happen to you. Don't let her win.*

Yeah, that's what he needed to be thinking about right now—how his dad seemed always to know the right thing to say. He'd known when to be tough, when to listen. He'd inspired Atticus to focus on his work and earn one of the highest case-solved records in KCPD this past year. That conversation still seemed fresh. And the pain of losing his dad to a murderer's bullets—when he allowed himself to think about it—felt fresher yet.

"Atticus?" He hadn't even been aware of squeezing his eyes shut, trying to hold on to the memory inside him. But he was more than aware of the nerves beneath his skin jumping at Brooke's gentle touch against his back. She pulled away as soon as he looked down over the jut of his shoulder at her. "It's okay to miss your father. I can't even remember mine and I still miss him sometimes. I didn't mean to upset you."

"I'm not."

"But the book—"

"I don't get upset. I do something about it." He sandwiched the journal between his hands and faced her. "May I borrow this?"

The concern on her face transformed into surprise, and then something else entirely as her gaze dropped to the middle of his tie and her cheeks pinked with color. "I was hoping to see if I could make sense of it first. Plus, I'd like to make sure there isn't anything too personal or… embarrassing… in it."

"I'll just look at the entries in Dad's handwriting."

"Please, Atticus." That bottom lip disappeared, then plumped back out in a wry half smile. "I write down a lot of stuff. Private stuff."

He supposed she had that right. It was *her* journal, after all. And after his experience with Hayley, he knew that there were secrets a woman liked to keep close to the vest. He had to believe that Brooke's secrets wouldn't come back to bite him in the ass the way Hayley's had.

"Of course." He reluctantly released the possible evidence when she pulled it from his grasp.

"I'll look through it tonight, and either cross things off or tear out the pages so you can see it tomorrow." She hugged the book to her chest. "You don't think I should turn it over to Detective Grove in Homicide, do you?"

"No." If he didn't get to analyze it right away, Grove didn't, either. "Let's not waste his time until we're sure it has something to do with Dad's murder."

Hell. He was snapping orders at her instead of sweet-talking her into letting him have that book. He hadn't brought her flowers, hadn't even remembered this was her first day in the precinct, hadn't given her any reason beyond her loyalty to his father to help him find answers—if there were any in that journal.

Ignoring the impulse to snatch the book from her hands, Atticus opted for a calmer, more cooperative approach. "Let's look through it together—bounce ideas off each other. You figured out his scribblings for five years, and I know my dad." Yes. This was shaping into a plan that could salve his guilty conscience as well as help his unofficial investigation. "Have you had lunch yet? It's my treat."

"You're asking me out?" She adjusted her glasses on her nose, squinting as though she hadn't heard him quite right. "Today? But I—"

A knock on the door interrupted his rebuttal.

"Is this Mr. Taylor's office?"

Atticus turned to the man wearing a white shirt, new carpenter's jeans and a visitor's pass. "Major Taylor isn't here right now. If you need assistance, the sergeant's desk is straight on down the hall."

"Miss Hansford?" Their visitor didn't budge.

"He's here for me." Brooke skirted around Atticus, taking the journal beyond his reach. "I can't go with you today. I'm afraid I already have plans."

Of all the stupid times to have a date. There was work to be done.

Wait a second. Brooke? Date?

The announcement bounced around the familiar world inside his head like a pinball machine. Not that she couldn't have a social life; he'd just never known her to. Of course, what did he really know about her personal life? Or her taste in men? This slicked-down six-footer wasn't exactly the professor or accountant he'd picture her with. Maybe there was something to that old adage about the quiet ones being unpredictable.

Wearing one of those rare smiles that brightened her features if a man noticed such things, Brooke extended her hand. "Mr. Fierro?"

"Call me Tony."

"I'm Brooke." She turned to include Atticus. "This is Detective Kincaid. Tony Fierro."

Introductions. Not a date. But his sigh of relief chilled in his lungs as he shook hands. This guy had a callused grip that was all wiry muscle despite pushing forty. The greenish-blue hints of tattoos peeking out from the cuffs of both sleeves gave a strong indication of why Fierro had so much time to work out. Atticus wasn't normally a betting man, but he'd wager that Fierro had a record. Was he here to do some kind of community service?

But Brooke eliminated that possibility, too. "I'm interviewing him for a job at the house—to do some handyman and yard work."

Despite the hushed, slightly hoarse timbre to his voice, Fierro wore a chip on his shoulder that was evident in the swagger of his posture. "Sorry I'm a little late, ma'am. I got turned around with some construction detours."

"Thanks for agreeing to stop by the office. There's been too much going on today for me to be able to get away."

He nodded. "I've had days like that."

"There's a deli down in the next block. I thought we

could order lunch in and conduct the interview here." She waved her hand toward one of the visitor chairs at her desk. "If that's okay with you. Having all these cops around doesn't make you uncomfortable, does it?"

Cops made this guy nervous? Atticus's suspicions ratcheted up another notch.

"I'm cool if you want to stay here."

"Great. Well. Give me a sec and I'll call in the order."

Atticus blocked Fierro at the door while Brooke hurried back to her desk. She disappeared for a moment before standing up with her shoes in one hand and her purse in the other.

After slipping into her sensible heels, she propped her purse open on top of the desk and started to dig. "I know I have a card for the deli in here somewhere."

While Brooke searched, Atticus sized up the Tony Fierro beneath the polished facade he'd put on for a potential employer. This guy was hiding something that Brooke might be too trusting to detect, but that Atticus was determined to uncover. Long-sleeved white shirt, still creased from the package it had come in. Buttoned up to the collar and down to the cuffs. On a muggy July day? That brown dye-job on his hair was fresh, too. Hadn't done as neat a job masking his light-colored eyebrows. And were those contact lenses he wore?

"Is there a problem, detective?" asked Fierro, his voice too low for Brooke to hear.

"I'm wondering how you got this meeting with Miss Hansford."

"It's a reintegration-into-the-community program. I've done odd jobs before for the company redoing her house. Haven't had any complaints. What are you, her secretary?"

Atticus pulled back the front of his jacket and propped his hands at his waist, giving Tony Smart-Mouth a clear view of the badge clipped to his belt, as well as the gun holstered there. "I'm a friend. A good one."

Fierro met Atticus's probing gaze, then turned his eyes beyond him to Brooke. "Relax, *friend*. All I'm after is the job. If you want to see my references, I'd be happy to give them to you, too. Otherwise, get out of my face. I need the work."

"What would you like to eat?" As Brooke held the business card in triumph, she dropped the journal into the bottomless pit of her bag. Their silence must have been a dead giveaway to the tension brewing between the two men because Brooke's smile quickly faded. Her eyes wide with concern, Brooke ushered Fierro into one of the chairs and, with a light touch at his elbow, nudged Atticus out into the hallway.

"Sorry. This is business I need to take care of. I won't forget about the journal. I promise."

"Brooke, wait." Atticus braced one hand against the door when she would have shut him out. His bold insistence surprised him almost as much as the propriety grip he held on her upper arm.

She looked up expectantly. What was he supposed to say? *Don't lock yourself in with this guy. Don't hire him. Stop wasting your smiles on him.* But Brooke was a grown woman, perfectly capable of making her own decisions about men, be they dates or employees or ex-cons, as he expected Fierro to be. It was probably just brotherly concern—looking out for his kid sister and all. Or maybe he was feeling antsy about the possibilities hidden in the journal that seemed forever lost to him in the bottom of the bag. What if this loser stole her purse? Trusting her judgment for the moment, Atticus released her. "When will you be finished with your meeting? I'd like to take a closer look at that item you showed me."

Her expression shuttered. "About forty-five minutes, give or take."

"I'll call you in an hour, then." Over the top of Brooke's head, he directed a pointed look at Fierro. *Yeah, buddy, I'll be checking to make sure that she's safe and sound after you leave.*

With a nod that didn't necessarily mean he'd heed the warning, Fierro turned and settled back in his chair. "Nice to meet you, *friend.*"

Atticus watched Brooke close the door, shutting herself in with the potential trouble. What could he do beyond a fit that would embarrass Brooke and make him come off like some kind of Neanderthal? Cramming his fists into the pockets of his slacks, Atticus headed back to the detectives' squad room on the main floor in the opposite direction.

Bravo for her willingness to give a man a second chance. That took a lot of heart and a lot of guts. But he wasn't quite ready to give Fierro the benefit of the doubt.

Atticus returned to his desk just long enough to run a check through the KCPD database. The information on Anthony Fierro was sketchy enough to raise a red flag. He'd served a dime in Jefferson City for robbery and related arms and assault charges. No rape or molestation charges against women or children. No murder.

That should have been a relief.

He glanced down the hallway toward Brooke's closed office.

"ARE YOU in?"

Antonio lowered the weights for one more rep and pressed the bar up and onto its braces before sitting up. Late at night was usually his time, when he was off the clock and could be himself and not have to answer to anybody. But tonight, his employer had stopped in for an unexpected visit. He couldn't tell if this meeting had to do with impatience or distrust. Either one smacked at his ego. He wasn't just good at what he did. He was the best.

"I'm in." Swinging his legs over the side of the weight bench, Tony reached for a towel and mopped the sweat from his forehead and sensitive eyes. "The bitch feels sorry for me. Thinks she's giving me a second chance. She completely trusts the recommendation from McCarthy. And he trusts yours."

He had to laugh. Brooke Hansford was naive about the world, a rare quality for a woman in her late twenties. She lived in a church with two spinster aunts for damn sake. She was anxious to help and eager to please, which made her putty in his manipulative hands. She wasn't much to look at—nothing wrong with her, just nothing to catch a man's eye. But he'd bet the six-figure paycheck he was making on this job that she was a virgin.

And plain or not, that added a fresh allure to the woman that he found mighty damn tempting. He dragged the towel slowly across his lips. Mighty tempting, indeed.

"Covering up your…indiscretions…was an expensive

investment. As if you weren't already freak enough." The jab at his albino genes jerked him away from his lascivious imaginings as if his employer could read his thoughts. "Don't disappoint me."

Where the hell do you think those freaky genes came from? He wanted to shout. But that wasn't how this relationship worked. Out loud he kept things purely business. "I said I got the job. Despite a little interference from another one of those Kincaid boys. I start tomorrow morning. If it's at her house, I'll find it. I have a plan for expanding the search elsewhere, as well."

His companion maintained a noticeable distance while Antonio wiped the sweat from his chest. "Don't be so damn cocky. Kincaid's sons are turning out to be an unpredictable threat. Instead of taking a leave of absence and following departmental rules, Sawyer Kincaid made that whole April fiasco personal—and I had specifically hand-picked those men to carry out my orders. It's not an easy thing to break a man out of prison. I thought Ace Longbow could handle Sawyer Kincaid for me, but I underestimated his obsession with his ex-wife."

A rare mistake for a plan that had been nearly thirty years in the making. "I've been your go-to man for a lot of years. You should have trusted me, not the new blood from prison. I had to take Longbow out myself. He was about to tell the cops everything he knew about us during that hostage standoff. Instead of eliminating the problem, he became the problem. All because of a woman."

"Yes, that was most unfortunate. I could have used a man with Longbow's skills."

Antonio's hand fisted around the towel with the urge to

either throw it or loop it around the boss's neck and squeeze until the criticisms stopped. Where was the loyalty? Antonio Fierro had provided those very same skills—reconnaissance, interrogation, intimidation, even murder—for six years. Just like his old man before him. Had the operation grown that large? Or was he, like Longbow and the two other prisoners they'd helped escape from a courthouse in Jefferson City earlier in the spring, expendable?

He forced himself to open his crushing grip and drop the towel, understanding that losing his temper with the boss was not something many people walked away from. Still, it rankled that he'd had to prove himself to the organization time and time again. So he had a little sideline that got him into trouble on occasion. He'd never failed an assignment.

He pushed away from the bench and moved to the rack of dumbbells, where he took his time selecting a challenging enough weight. "I wouldn't worry about this other Kincaid brother. He's not romantically involved with Brooke Hansford. He's a badge through and through. I can work around that. I'll find it."

"We're not even sure what we're looking for yet. A disk? A notebook? Even a video or tape recording. John Kincaid was right to suspect that we were still in business, and his inside information could destroy us."

His boss's paranoia was growing tiresome. But then, how did one survive—and succeed—for so many years without detection unless there was some degree of constant suspicion involved? He had to respect the success—and the opportunity to make enough money to buy himself a tax-free retirement in the Caribbean.

"What if the Hansford chick doesn't have it?"

"She must. Even if she doesn't know it. Kincaid took a keen interest in her purchase of that house and in the woman herself, more so than any employer typically would have. That has to mean something."

"Maybe they were having an affair," Tony suggested, "and the house was going to be their love nest. She was crying at the funeral."

The idea seemed to be a source of amusement. "Not John. The age difference probably isn't an issue these days, but you can take one look at her and know she's not a mankiller." Antonio grinned. Maybe Kincaid had been into virgins, too. But the boss was talking, so he made an effort to listen. "He made a cop's salary, so you know she wasn't a gold-digger. And I knew John Kincaid. He was ridiculously, boringly, completely married to his wife. No fun at all."

Another possible explanation for Kincaid's interest in Brooke Hansford hit uncomfortably close to home. "What if she's his daughter? It wouldn't be the first time a parent refused to acknowledge an illegitimate child. I know others who—" he slid a glance across the room "—look out for their children without ever claiming them."

There was not even one flicker of recognition in that expression. His boss was one cool customer. "She is Leo and Irina's daughter. John would have known that. Perhaps that's the key. He took her under his wing since he was responsible, in part, for what happened to them. Poor John had a guilty conscience about leaving her an orphan." The boss smiled behind steepled fingers. "That makes me more certain than ever that he'd want to clear that conscience before he died."

"Whatever." Antonio started his biceps curls while his

visitor pulled out his Smart Phone and touched the stylus to the screen, probably completing a transaction some-place across the world that would make millions of dollars with a single stroke of a pen—or maybe handing out an as-signment to another employee. Yeah, he was mixin' it up with some pretty influential company these days. He deserved to be a part of this.

With the message sent, the electronic device went back inside the tailored jacket. "I've exhausted every other avenue where Kincaid might have kept that information. My sources have come up with nothing. Do what's neces-sary to press Miss Hansford and find it."

Squeezing his biceps until his audience lost interest, Antonio resumed the conversation. Each dumbbell hit the rack with an ominous portent. "All right. Say Kincaid did write down the details—and I find them. The Cold War has been over for a long time. Is there anybody left who really cares?"

"*I* care." The boss rose and headed toward the gym's exit where a bodyguard was standing watch. "I always wanted my name exonerated. And since that can never happen, I at least want the people who forced me into this double life to pay."

John Kincaid had paid with his life. So had others. There were plans for more. Tony had no intention of joining the list. "I have a stake in this, too. When Irina Zorinsky *died*, my birthright died, too. Somebody has to pay for that." Antonio moved closer, dared to bring his sweaty, smelly self into his boss's personal space.

But if he expected to get a rise, he was dead wrong. This was one cold customer. Without even a blink, the order was reconfirmed. "I want that information."

Antonio wisely retreated a step. "Understood."

His employer buttoned and smoothed an already neat jacket. "And I want answers before you find your satisfaction."

"Don't worry. She's not my type."

"She's female, isn't she? Aren't they all your type?"

Eventually. If he wanted them to be. Antonio headed for the showers. "The girl's not gonna be a problem."

Chapter Five

Looking through his binoculars from the driveway at the end of the street, Atticus watched the idyllic summer scene unfold behind Brooke's stone house. "Now there's irony for you."

He was in the doghouse for butting his nose into Brooke's business yesterday—at least that's what he believed the finger pointing over his roast beef sandwich and breathless, *You... you... I'm a grown woman. You don't have to...oh, just stay away and let me make my own decisions!* meant.

Meanwhile, Tony Fierro seemed to be the golden boy. The ex-con was leaning on a shovel in Brooke's backyard, laughing over something her Aunt Louise said. And her Aunt Peggy was serving them glasses of lemonade—probably the really cold stuff, more tart than sweet—while Atticus sat here, parched, with beads of sweat trickling down the small of his back.

He could turn on the engine of his silver SUV and crank the air conditioning, but a running vehicle drew more attention than a parked one, and the open windows gave him a clearer view of Fierro and Louise digging in the weedy garden. And since he didn't imagine that being caught spying on Brooke a second time—even if she was at work this morning and he was only, technically, spying on her house—would earn him points toward forgiveness and a chance to sit down with her and read that journal, he opted for flying under the radar rather than being cool and comfortable.

The soaring temperature on the cloudless day wasn't the only thing fueling the warmth in his veins. He kept replaying that little scene outside her office.

He'd been amused at first by the uncharacteristic show of defiance. Her words had tumbled out faster than her temper, and her cheeks had colored a healthy shade of pink, adding fire to her lecture and vibrancy to her entire posture. But when he realized that she saw his concern as interference—maybe even an insult—and that this unfamiliar independent streak meant he wasn't meeting with her or the journal that afternoon, then Atticus countered with a pithy comeback. *Maybe if you showed better judgment in the men you want to spend time with, then I wouldn't have to babysit you.*

So he'd never been privy to the easy charm that Holden and Sawyer enjoyed. He knew better than that how to talk to a twenty-nine-year-old woman.

Babysit. He'd been idiot enough to actually use that word with Brooke.

He could have sworn she wanted to slap his face.

Not one of his finer moments.

He'd never imagined that Brooke Hansford had a temper. He'd never dreamed that, of all people, *she* could make him lose his.

He was paying for that slipup today.

Figuratively cooled off after twenty-four hours, Atticus settled back into the familiar role of a detective. Brooke and her aunts were like family. They'd decided to hire an ex-con to fix their garden and who knew what else. It was out of a sense of duty that he was following up to make sure Tony Fierro had reformed enough to deserve their trust.

All the red flags were there to say otherwise. The get-out-of-my-face attitude yesterday. The bandanna covering the bad hair job today. And even from this distance Atticus could see that, stripped down to a white T-shirt in deference to the heat, Fierro's tats were definitely prison issue. Apparently, he'd been a petty criminal in his life before prison, and minor thefts and burglaries had escalated into a series of convenience store armed robberies. Whether those were the extent of his crimes, or more serious charges had been pled down in order to secure a conviction, the records didn't say.

The records didn't say much about Fierro before his life of crime, either. Another red flag.

Atticus raised the binoculars again when the back door opened and another man came out of the house. Atticus recognized him as Truman McCarthy, the contractor overseeing the church's remodelling. McCarthy and his men were working inside this afternoon. But now he jumped off the edge of the unfinished deck and walked over to shake Fierro's hand. Atticus had checked him out, too. Reputable businessman. Self-made success. He often hired former convicts or teen offenders for non-union labor on his building projects. His way of giving back to the community, Atticus supposed. Though he couldn't tell what they were saying, McCarthy's body language indicated a comfortable, familiar relationship with Fierro. The boss merited a glass of lemonade, too.

Damn, it was hot to be working surveillance today.

Atticus lowered his binoculars, unbuttoned his collar and loosened his tie. Maybe the cases he'd worked over the years, along with Hayley's betrayal, had made him just too damn cynical. His father's unsolved murder made him look at everyone as suspect. McCarthy was a respected member of the community. If his approval of Fierro was enough for Brooke, it should be enough for him. He was worrying too much about this guy, trying to prove his instincts were right and Brooke's were wrong.

Besides, Brooke was safely at work downtown, surrounded by dozens of cops, working under the very watchful eye of his superior, Mitch Taylor. He didn't even have a good enough excuse to sit here and watch over Brooke's aunts. With McCarthy and his men in and out of the house from sunup to dusk, there would be plenty of activity here to keep Fierro on his good behavior. And if he continued to work outside, there'd be no opportunity at all for him to help himself to anything of the Hansfords. Atticus was just being overly cautious because if something happened to Brooke's journal, then he'd never get a look inside the pages to see if his father really had been trying to send a message to the future.

Deciding to give Brooke and Fierro the benefit of the doubt—for now—Atticus started the engine and adjusted the air conditioning to its highest setting. He was pulling into city traffic when the phone on his belt rang.

He checked the number, then flipped it open. "Hey, Sawyer. What's up?"

Big brother didn't waste time with any greeting. "I heard Kevin Grove is bringing in the witness who called in Dad's murder for another interview today. That may mean there's been a break on the case. Marcus Henry is running the camera in the recording booth. I convinced him to let us sit in and watch. I'll round up Holden, too, if he's not on a call. Can you meet me there?"

Atticus was already in the passing lane, pushing harder on the gas. "I'm on my way."

"Mirza?" Brooke looked up from the memo she was typing and smiled at the dark-skinned man lugging a big leather satchel through her doorway. "You're the computer guy? They said Caldwell Technologies would be sending someone to train me on their software today, but I had no idea it'd be you. I haven't seen you since our last class at UMKC."

Mirza Patel brushed his curly black hair off his cheek and tucked it behind his ear. "To be honest, I volunteered. My supervisor says I will never get a raise if I cannot show the company that I can leave my cubicle and work with customers. When I saw your name, I thought of what we learned in class."

Brooke was on her feet, circling the desk. "When you go into an unfamiliar situation, take baby steps. Plan so that not everything is completely new. New face? Familiar place."

"New place? Familiar face." His satchel thunked on the floor beside him as he finished the rhyme of advice from the assertiveness training they'd taken together. "You are my familiar face here."

An impulse to welcome her friend with a hug became an awkward dodge of arms that ended with a firm handshake. "I'm happy to be your safety net. You can be my familiar face for a while, too. There are so many new people here, it can be a bit overwhelming." She pulled him on into her office and gestured to her desk. "There's my computer. I've been reading the manual, but I'm looking forward to a hands-on demo."

While Mirza took a few minutes to set up, Brooke pulled a visitor's chair around to the same side of the desk so she'd be able to observe the tutorial. "I understand Caldwell tailored this particular program to suit the needs of the police department."

Mirza's Indian accent was almost musical as he explained, "It is very similar to the word processing and database program we have created for military use. Of course, this is on a smaller scale. It allows you to create a network within the department, as well as access offsite systems while converting incoming information to a standard format."

"That should save me a few steps."

"It also includes neighborhood, city and state maps with resident and business addresses, as well as templates for spreadsheets, presentations and word processing, like the memo you are typing."

"Oh." Brooke reached over his shoulder. "Let me print that out and get it on Major Taylor's desk. Then you can reboot the system and we can start." After laying the memo in Mitch Taylor's inbox to be initialed, Brooke returned to find Mirza plugging in cords and a router and typing in commands. "You said Caldwell based this system on a military program?"

"Yes. Caldwell Tech has worked very closely with the

Department of Defense for nearly thirty years, developing various technologies for them. It has only been twelve years since Mr. Caldwell created the civilian division of the company. That is where I work, of course." He gestured to the extra chair. "Are you ready to begin?"

Two HOURS and several pages of notes later, Brooke had a good working knowledge of the new computer systems. She also had a serious crick in her neck.

She could probably attribute the stiffness to more than just hunching over the computer. She'd been worrying since she'd left the house that morning about how well her aunts were getting along with the new handyman that Atticus had been so opposed to hiring.

As if a twenty-nine-year-old woman couldn't make a grown-up decision on her own!

Sure, maybe she was a little uncomfortable with his criminal record, but Tony Fierro had served his time. He hadn't threatened her in any way. His record since his release was clean and the recommendation from Mr. McCarthy couldn't be more glowing. On paper, there was absolutely no reason she shouldn't hire Tony to do odd jobs around the house. And in the end, she relied on the facts, rather than her questionable intuition, to make her decision to give him the job.

"Sorry, but I need a break." She stretched her neck this way and that. Maybe she should send Mirza for coffee in the break room while she phoned Peggy and Lou. "Do you mind?"

"Of course not." Mirza stood when Brooke did, and did a little stretching himself. "We work well together."

"We sure do." Brooke reached up to rub her neck.

"Turns out you're a very good teacher. You should leave your cubicle more often," she teased.

"Perhaps I will." Mirza's hands joined hers at the nape of her neck and massaged lightly. Brooke froze at the unexpected contact. "Is…this all right?"

"Um…" Mirza was a friend. As shy as she was. It had probably cost him as much nerve to reach out to her as it had to venture into customer service at Caldwell. A rejection from her right now would probably knock his confidence back a notch or two. Brooke forced herself to relax. "That's fine. Maybe a little farther out on the shoulders," she suggested, hoping to lessen that awkwardly intimate feeling.

Mirza's touch grew more firm as the massage continued. One hand circled around her collarbone to provide a counterbalance as he worked the butt of his hand along her spine. Brooke silently began to count to ten. Then she'd find an excuse to remove herself from his touch without hurting his feelings.

Six. Seven.

"Mail."

Thank God. When the intern rolled his mail cart through her doorway, Brooke slipped around the desk and greeted him with an enthusiastic hi. She didn't turn to see if Mirza had noticed the abruptness of her escape. She didn't want to know if his offer of a massage was just a friendly gesture or an unwelcome overture to something more.

Brooke kept her gaze purposefully lowered as she sorted through the mail. If Mirza saw her as nothing more than a friend, then he wouldn't be offended by the loss of eye contact. If there was some unrequited feeling on his part, however, then she was giving him an easy way to avoid embarrassing himself.

"I'd better get this taken care of," she explained needlessly.

"Yes. And I suppose I had better pack my things and get back to Caldwell." The weird moment passed and Mirza sat to put away his equipment.

But a weird moment with Mirza Patel was the least of Brooke's problems.

According to Mitch's directions, she had permission to open each letter and prioritize them. But as she slit open one envelope and unfolded the parchment inside, all the other papers fell to the floor, unheeded. "This can't be."

A sick confusion twisted in her stomach. Why was this happening to her?

She pulled off her glasses as if reading the strange missive up close to her nearsighted eyes would make it more understandable.

Did you get the roses, pretty lady?
I wanted you to know I'm thinking of you. All the time.
See you soon.

Slipping her glasses back into place, Brooke dropped to her knees and searched through the scattered papers to find the envelope the anonymous note had come in. She snatched it up and read it more carefully. Kansas City postmark. Prepaid envelope with no licked stamp. Addressed to Mitch Taylor's office at the Fourth Precinct, attention Brooke Hansford. No return address.

"Is everything all right, Brooke?"

Ignoring her friend's concern, Brooke pushed to her

feet and darted into the hall to catch the intern, but he'd already disappeared. Her heart thumped in her chest as she looked down the empty corridor to the vacant bank of elevators, and then turned to the busy squad room, wondering if someone was watching her now, wondering if anyone thought this was funny.

But no one was laughing. No one was paying any attention to her at all except…

Brooke dashed back into her office. "Mirza. Did you send me flowers yesterday?"

Please let it be this man's misguided expression of his attraction to her.

"Me? Flowers?"

Before his gaping mouth could say no, Brooke went to the bookshelf and picked up the glass vase with the six red roses. "Do you have a girlfriend, Mirza?"

"No."

"Boyfriend?"

"No!"

"Mother?"

"She is visiting from India this summer."

Good enough. Brooke pushed the vase into his hands. "Here. Take these. Impress her. And for God's sake, sign a card when you give them to her."

"YOU THINK that color's natural?" Holden rolled the sleeves of his black S.W.A.T. uniform up past his elbows and pointed to the computer monitor, indicating Liza Parrish's tomboyishly short wisps of copper-colored hair on the television screen. She wore layered tank tops, cargo shorts and an attitude that radiated off her freckled skin. She sat alone in the interview room, alternately drumming her fingers against the metal tabletop and sneaking peeks at the wall clock—as though she knew an observation camera was hidden there. "The freckles look authentic, but that red's not something you pass by without looking twice."

"Missing the point, little brother." Sawyer rose from his perch on the table in the back of the observation room and nudged Holden aside. "She's here to answer questions, not help you get your game on. Now sit—" There was an audible pause in the good-natured ribbing. "How old is she? What the hell was a kid like that doing down at the docks in the middle of the night?"

Atticus hadn't met the witness who'd called in John Kincaid's murder in person, but he had the stats memorized. "She's twenty-five. A veterinary school grad student. Claims she was rescuing a dog for a friend."

"By herself in the middle of the night?" Holden nudged back to get a better look. "Is she smart enough for us to trust anything she says? Or do you think she's lying?"

Technician Marcus Henry sat between them, making adjustments on his keyboard and shaking his head. "Dinners at your mom's house must have been a laugh a minute with the three of you growing up."

Sawyer thumped him on the back of the head. "Just see if you ever rate an invitation now. And there were four of us. Edward added plenty of noise of his own, believe me."

"I haven't seen Ed around the precinct since last December. Or was that two Christmases ago? Has he recovered from his—" Marcus tapped his headphones. "Wait. Grove's coming in. Keep it down."

Another man with Atticus's temperament might have

shushed the Two Stooges by now. But he knew his brothers. When it was time to get serious, the games would stop. Gathering behind Marcus as they watched Detective Kevin Grove enter the interrogation room, the Kincaid brothers were at once as focused and serious as the grave.

"Who's that?" Atticus pointed to the tall, slender woman who followed the stocky detective into the room.

Sawyer answered. "The crime lab's resident battleax, Holly Masterson. Not much of a people person, but thorough. She's the M.E. I told you about who called me to report that some of her computer records had been tampered with—including Dad's autopsy."

Atticus filed away the information, keeping his eyes glued to the screen. Grove waited for Dr. Masterson to take a seat at the end of the table before sitting across from Liza Parrish himself. He raked his fingers through his spiky blond hair and took a deep breath as though this had already been a very long day for him. He pulled a small tape recorder from his jacket and placed it on the table.

"Let's get the formalities out of the way first, Miss Parrish. You remember me, Detective Grove. This is Holly Masterson from the crime lab. We're here to interview Liza Parrish regarding the homicide of Deputy Commissioner John Kincaid. You've waived your right to have an attorney present and we'll be taping the interview. Do you understand all this?"

The redhead nodded.

"I need you to state it out loud for the recorder, Miss Parrish."

The drumming of her fingers stopped and she sat up straight. "Yes. I understand. You know, I'm missing work for this. The animal clinic's short-staffed as it is, so could we get on with it?"

"Of course." Grove's build resembled a heavyweight wrestler's, putting his physical appearance at odds with his precise, articulate manner of speaking. "Dr. Masterson has pulled a tattoo from a victim we believe is related to the murder you witnessed."

Liza rolled her eyes and leaned back. "For the umpteenth time, I didn't actually *see* the murder. I saw people driving away in the car, and when I went inside the warehouse I found the body and called 911. I didn't stay because my dog needed medical attention and there was nothing I could do for that poor man—"

"I thought it was a friend's dog." Holden pointed out the first inconsistency in her story.

"Shh," Atticus warned.

"—but I gave the dispatcher my cell phone number and home address in case KCPD needed to reach me."

Grove nodded. "We appreciate your assistance, Miss Parrish. But we have a new angle on the case we'd like to discuss."

Atticus's fingers tightened at his waist as he braced for the revelation.

Grove nodded to Dr. Masterson, who slid a manila envelope in front of Liza. "Does the number three have any significance to what you saw?" he asked.

Three? Alert to every word spoken on the monitor, Atticus opened a sidebar of memory in his head. He'd seen a number three on the drawing his father had sketched in Brooke's journal. Did it mean something important?

"Huh?" Liza Parrish wasn't sure of the answer, either.

"There were three people there, I guess. The white guy driving the car. The big black man holding the back door open. And the suit who was climbing inside."

Dr. Masterson interrupted, a little less woman-to-woman in her approach than Atticus would have expected. She opened the envelope and pulled out a photograph. "We're talking about the number three being used as a symbol. Like a gang tat that shows affiliation. Did you notice this on any of the men you saw driving away?"

"That's a tattoo?" Liza asked, leaning in to study the picture and crinkling her face up into a frown. "Oh, my God. Is this guy dead, too?"

"Yes. His name was James McBride…"

Sawyer turned to whisper in Atticus's ear. "Masterson told me she saw a tattoo on Dad's body. Almost microscopic in size. She overlooked it as a birthmark in the initial autopsy."

"A number three?"

"Must have been. She said the markings were similar."

Holden pushed his way into the conversation, too. "I never knew Dad had a tat."

It was news to Atticus, too. "None of us did."

Holly Masterson was still talking about the victim. "…a retired accountant at Caldwell Technologies. I've magnified the image to make it easier to see. Does the tattoo look familiar?"

Atticus tapped Marcus on the shoulder. "Can we adjust the camera to see that photo?"

"Are you kidding? You're lucky you're getting to see it from this angle."

"It's hard to tell on the dark skin." Liza Parrish tapped

her freckled chin. "The albino guy driving the car had tats all over him. But, you know, from my hiding place behind the trash cans, I didn't get that good a look at him to see anything like this. It's too tiny."

Tattoos.

Albino.

Bad dye job.

The blood drained to Atticus's feet. A surge of adrenaline followed right behind. "Son of a bitch."

"Atticus?"

The door swung open before Atticus could reach it.

Mitch Taylor was not the man you wanted to see blocking your path if you were in a hurry. "What the hell are you three doing in here? Your father's homicide is strictly off limits and you know it." He thumbed over his shoulder, ordering them out of the observation room. "Unless you want to be directing traffic tomorrow, you get out of here now. And you," he pointed to Marcus, "I'll see you in my office when that interview is done."

"Yes, sir."

Mitch grabbed Atticus's arm on the way out. His voice dropped several decibel levels. "I'll keep you in the loop if anything comes from this interview. But you and your brothers stay away from this case. When we nail John's killer, I don't want the perp walking on a technicality like personal prejudice from a detective."

"You're right. Having a guilty man go free might be worse than never catching him at all."

"We'll catch him," Mitch vowed. "But you and your brothers can't be a part of this. Now, you're the reasonable one. Talk some sense into them."

Reasonable, hell. If he was so damn smart, why hadn't he figured out this case yet?

Atticus kept the frustration locked inside him and nodded. "We appreciate any information you can give us. It just feels like it's taking far too long to get any answers. Homicide still hasn't turned up one viable suspect or motive, and forensics' evidence is inconclusive at best."

"You're preaching to the choir, A. We won't give up until we have our man."

"Neither will any of my brothers or myself."

"Speaking of brothers—" Mitch ushered him into the hallway and closed the door behind him. "Any idea when Edward is coming back? Or if he plans even to be a cop again? I know the best sometimes burn out and can't find their way back. I don't want to lose him, but I can't keep his position open forever."

"He knows that. When I get a chance, I'll see if I can find out where his head is right now."

"You do that and I'll pretend I never saw you here."

With a final "Yes, sir," Atticus hurried off to make sure Brooke hadn't made a dangerous—even fatal—mistake in hiring Tony Fierro.

And whether his interference sparked her temper or not, he intended to meet Tony Fierro face-to-face and find out if those were brown contact lenses over colorless—albino—eyes.

Chapter Six

"I mean anything. No detail is too small. What street did he live on growing up? Did he run with a gang? Sing in the choir? Anything you can tell me." Atticus held his cell phone to his ear and nodded to friends as members of B shift walked past his desk, getting ready for the night watch. He'd meant to check out himself half an hour ago, but these phone calls were too important to wait for the morning.

He pulled off his reading glasses and rubbed at his temple when the clerk in Kansas City's FBI office reported that the information on Anthony Fierro in their database was just as sketchy as KCPD's. Her helpful suggestion only fueled his suspicions about the ex-con having erased at least parts of his past—or having someone with powerful connections do it for him.

The patrol car Atticus had requested to swing by Brooke's house for an hourly check while Fierro was there wouldn't be much of a deterrent for a man with connections like that. There was something bigger, deeper, going on here. Was he some kind of mob or government informant with a new identity created through witness relocation?

Was he a deeply embedded terrorist plant? Or was he just a run-of-the-mill criminal who'd paid big bucks to make parts of his life disappear? None of those scenarios would be good news for Brooke. And none of them explained any kind of link Fierro might have had with his father.

"No. The Department of Corrections directed me to you." The D.A.'s search had been a bust as well. Maybe he needed to expand this to an international search—but that would mean a lot of red tape and a lot of man-hours based on little more than coincidence and his gut. "Yes. Flag it," he agreed when the offer was made. "This guy's flying under the radar. No one who served ten years in Jeff City can be that squeaky clean before going in. Yeah. Keep me posted if you turn up anything." He wasn't holding his breath. "Thanks."

Almost the instant he hung up, his cell phone vibrated, indicating an incoming text message. "Look up" it said.

He did.

Ah, yes. The icing on the cake of a truly crappy day.

The platinum blonde closed her phone, smiling a little too perfectly for Atticus's taste as she pulled away from the cubicle wall where she'd been lounging and crossed to his desk. "Long time, no see, stranger."

"Hayley." Atticus stood, not out of polite habit, he told himself, but because it was time to leave. He rolled down the sleeves of his shirt and buttoned the cuffs. "I'm on my way out."

The excuse was as genuine as it was improvised. He needed to see Brooke—see for himself that her decision to bring Fierro into her life wasn't one she regretted already. And if she'd forgiven him for overstepping the bounds of big brotherhood yesterday, then he wanted to look at her journal. Besides, a little of that peace and calm his dad had found so appealing about Brooke sounded pretty enticing right about now.

Hayley perched on the chair beside his desk. "Saying hi like civilized people doesn't take that long, does it?"

It did when the person saying hi made his skin crawl with mistrust. "I'm a busy man."

She brushed her bangs aside with the tip of her pinkie. "Then I'll approach this as a professional rather than an old friend."

To his way of thinking, Hayley Resnick didn't qualify as either. Atticus pulled his jacket from the back of his chair and slipped into it. Man, he needed a good dose of something to curb his sarcastic thoughts. "I'm just a working cop. Talk to the press liaison."

"About your father's murder?"

"What about it?" He buttoned his collar and straightened the knot of his tie, pretending every nerve in his body hadn't just gone on full alert.

"I understand you brought in a potential witness for questioning this afternoon."

"I didn't do anything. It's not my case."

"You're telling me that after three months, KCPD doesn't have any new leads? No suspect? No motive?"

He pointed across several groupings of desks to where Kevin Grove was still working. "The big, blond guy. Detective Grove. He's running the investigation. Talk to him."

She stepped into his path when he headed to the sign-out board. "No tit for tat anymore?" He didn't even flinch when she stroked her fingers along his lapel. "Our relationship wasn't completely about our jobs, Atticus. It doesn't have to be this way between us."

She wasn't getting the name of the witness, or even confirmation that Liza Parrish existed. She wasn't getting any mention about a microscopic tattoo. And she sure as hell wasn't finding out about Brooke or the journal. Not from him.

He plucked her hand away. "That story you used to scoop your way onto the number-one news show in KC? It led to the compromise of a safe house I was guarding. I was drugged when the house was attacked, the witness nearly killed. And, by the way, where were you while I was in the hospital recovering? Typing up your notes?"

"Don't be mean, sweetheart. I didn't know you were hurt. Of course, I would have left the station to visit you if I had known." Her rose-tinted lips trembled right on cue, as if she thought that apologetic pout would soften him up.

Wrong. "The partner I was working with sold out because your story told the mob where to put their money. That falls on my head, *sweetheart*."

"The witness survived because you warned her before passing out. The bad guys are dead or in prison. You're still a cop. No harm, no foul."

Talk about missing the point. "You're not getting diddly squat from me." He thumbed over his shoulder, as he pushed his way past her toward Brooke's office. "Talk to Grove."

Leaving Hayley to work her dubious charms on the other detective, Atticus strode down the hallway toward Brooke's office. He supposed he could have asked Hayley to use her connections to see if she could find out anything about Tony Fierro's neat and tidy past. But that was a source of information he'd never trust again. His own search had yielded nothing more than a recently issued driver's license and a birth certificate so poorly copied that Fierro's father could have been *Ivan* or *Luanne* or *Unknown*.

But he wasn't about to give up until he knew for certain there was no threat. Atticus Kincaid didn't say "uncle."

He slowed his steps as he neared Brooke's office. "Damn. Missed her."

Lights off. Nobody home.

He almost turned around except… A soft, shuffling sound drew him back against the wall to listen. He held his breath and paused a moment, quickly determining that that was no cleaning lady rummaging around inside. Reaching through the open doorway, Atticus flipped on the lights.

A man with curly black hair jumped in Brooke's chair.

Atticus stepped over the threshold. "Who are you?"

A drawer slammed shut and the man shot to his feet, sending the chair spinning back into the bookshelf, toppling notebooks. He stopped the spinning, then straightened and held up the visitor's pass around his neck. "Mirza Patel. I have permission to be here. Don't shoot."

Atticus didn't waste his time pointing out that his gun was still holstered, and moved into the center of the room. "That pass gives you permission to enter the building, not this office."

As he approached, he analyzed the intruder's average height, average build and—as an unusual side effect in an air-conditioned building—the beads of sweat dotting his upper lip.

"What are you doing here?" *Going through Brooke's things* went unspoken. The man reached down beside him.

"Keep your hands where I can see them." Or he *would* pull the damn gun.

Patel came back up with both hands high in the air. "I'm a computer technician from Caldwell Enterprises. I have been training Brooke on CT Software. We are friends, she and I. I left a cord when I packed up earlier today. I need it for my computer."

"Does she know you're here?"

"I didn't want her to know how forgetful I am." His face creased with a smile. "She gave me flowers when I left, which made me forget things. They were for my mother, she said, but I know…"

Glancing at the shelves behind the man, Atticus noted that the red roses were missing. He could tell that something about those flowers had bugged Brooke from the moment he'd brought them in yesterday. And now she'd passed them on to this guy? There was something wrong here, something Brooke wasn't telling him.

"…when we took the class together, I felt she was someone—"

Atticus interrupted his tale of his geek-love crush on Brooke. "Did you find your cord?"

Patel's smile vanished. "She must have put it away. I suppose I could get it when I come back tomorrow for the second day of her training."

"Good plan."

Understanding that that also meant goodbye and get out, Patel shuffled around the desk, doubling his pace as Atticus put his hand on the butt of his gun and followed him out the door.

Once the uninvited guest cleared the hallway, Atticus

returned to Brooke's office. He righted the notebooks and pushed her chair back up to the desk, then opened his phone to call her. "How'd I overlook that?"

She wasn't on his call list. It had never seemed important enough to carry her number with him, but now he wished he had her on speed dial.

It was a mistake he intended to rectify. Until then, "We'll do this the old-fashioned way." Plucking a sheet from her cube of notepaper, he pulled out a pen and wrote her a message.

We need to talk ASAP. If I don't catch you tonight,
please make time for me first thing tomorrow morning.
                                                    Atticus.

He set the note at the center of her calendar blotter. His search for a coffee mug or paperweight to anchor it there took his eye to the bottom left drawer of Brooke's desk, which hadn't closed completely because someone had jammed it in at an angle—as if that *someone* had been caught going through Brooke's things.

His gaze and thoughts drifted to the door. Was Mirza Patel really such a bumbling idiot? Or was that absent-minded professor act a sly cover?

Leaving nothing to speculation, Atticus unjammed the drawer and opened it. There were two boxes of computer disks inside, one with the cover not completely pulled back into place. The disks themselves were tilted in opposite directions, as though whoever had sorted through them had been interrupted part way through—or had found what he was looking for and stopped.

Had Patel been searching through these disks?

Had he found what he was looking for?

Atticus's gaze slid to the trash can beside her desk. Or was he looking for that? He fished out a half-crumpled letter. Typed. Plain paper. Simple message. Unsigned. Unremarkable in and of itself, except he'd seen Brooke's reaction to the flowers. They hadn't been a welcome gift.

See you soon.

A promise. Or a threat.

"What the hell's going on, Brooke? What aren't you telling me?"

Atticus folded the note and tucked it inside his jacket, turned off the lights and headed for the exit.

When had the quiet secretary who'd always blended into the background become such a complex woman of mystery? And why did this growing concern for all things Brooke keep nagging at him like a time bomb about to blow up in his face?

BROOKE HUGGED her purse to her chest, drawing into herself as she rode the elevator down to the main floor of the precinct building. She'd smiled a general acknowledgment to her companions in the elevator, but retreated to the back corner of the car while they carried on their conversations about their workday and evening plans.

She didn't want to talk to anyone right now—didn't want to have to worry about saying the right thing or dredging up the nerve to speak at all and pretend she wasn't as mentally and emotionally exhausted as she was feeling right now. She needed to be alone and find that quiet center of strength inside her again. She needed time to think and deal.

For a woman who had no love life to speak of—and who had learned to get along well enough without one, thank you very much—all this anonymous attention she'd been receiving felt more disturbing than flattering.

Was this someone's really bad idea of a joke? Torment the spinster chick until she breaks down into tears or finally blows her stack? That was a nasty flashback to middle school she didn't intend to relive.

Could there be a man out there—the secret admirer Atticus had teased her about—even more unskilled in the romance department than she? Too shy to sign his name or too nervous to remember the courtesy?

Or had she become the target of something much more sinister?

She wasn't sure if she was clinging to the leather bag because it was the only solid thing to hold on to for comfort, or if she was using it like a shield of armor. Not that it really mattered. Her bag might allow her to carry her daily survival kit around with her, but it provided neither the comfort nor the security she craved. A strong set of arms wrapped around her would be far better....

No. Don't go there, Hansford. There was no hero riding in on his white charger—or driving up in his silver SUV—to help her. She'd inherited strong independent genes from her aunts. She just needed a few quiet moments to regroup—to get past the watching and gifts and personal notes that no one would claim.

The elevator dinged and the doors parted before she was ready to face the world again. After checking out at the security desk and having her bag examined at the front gate, it was easy enough to revert to the habit of gluing her gaze to the sidewalk and avoiding eye contact with anyone. She made her way down the block and waited at the corner light with a small group of city workers to cross the street to the parking garage.

The sun was just beginning to set, but was still high enough on the horizon to warm her skin. She lifted her face to its sultry caress and breathed in deeply. She'd be all right. She'd get through this. There had to be some logical explanation that, once she figured it out, she'd be laughing about tomorrow.

By the time the light changed, she was holding her chin high and thanking the gentleman who invited her to precede him. When the group reached the parking garage, they fanned out, some heading to the elevator, others around the gate to their ground-level vehicles. Feeling fit if not completely fine after her internal down time, Brooke turned to the open stairs that ran up the southwest corner of the garage, keeping the sun on her shoulders and her positive thinking in place.

Perhaps it was the lingering heat of the day that made the sudden chill of the shadows when she entered the third-floor level so noticeable a shock that it raised goose bumps beneath the sleeves of her blouse. Shaking off the unexpected cold snap, Brooke lengthened her stride. She'd parked on the opposite end of the garage that morning, knowing that on busy days like this one, her walk to and from the car might be the only aerobic exercise she got.

A sudden breeze lifted her hair and tickled the back of her neck. She glanced quickly over her shoulder. The leaves on the trees outside the garage weren't moving.

Must be some trick of her imagination, or more likely, a mini-cyclone created by the variance between the hot and cool temps.

Brooke wrapped both fists around the shoulder strap of her bag and kept walking. She heard the chatter of men's voices from somewhere below her and found herself eavesdropping on their conversation. It made her feel a little less alone up here as she pulled out her keys and wondered why she'd thought parking so far away had sounded like a good idea this morning. She made out "Royals" and "Yankees" and pieces of a debate as to whether one's pitching could beat the other's hitting.

Catching a glimpse of movement from the corner of her eye, Brooke stuttered to a halt. What was that wisp of color she'd seen between those two trucks? There was nothing there now. Could a purplish bird have darted by?

Nervous energy tightened her throat to a whisper. "Name one purple bird."

Purple martin. Purple finch. Neither one was really purple in color. Maybe she wasn't so alone on the third level as she'd thought.

"Go." Her calf-length skirt swirled between her knees as she picked up the pace.

Gravel crunched beneath a footstep on the concrete behind her and Brooke jumped in her skin. That was one big damn purple bird. Before her heart thumped right out of her chest, she stopped. Swung around. Saw no one.

"Hello? Is someone there?" It would be a hell of a lot easier to confront her fear if she could actually see what was terrifying her. Her chest rose and fell as she took deep, steady breaths. Her knuckles whitened around her keys and purse. The only sounds now were the baseball fans on the level below her and her pulse pounding in her ears. "This isn't funny, you know. I'm not laughing."

The elevator pinged, announcing it had arrived on this floor and the doors were about to open. In her mind she tried to be sensible, tried to relax. *Wait for company. Wait until you're not alone. Wait...*

A man's laughter, low-pitched and mocking, echoed in the air around her.

"Oh, God." Brooke backed up, hit the center railing and spun around. Fear turned her legs to jelly and she stumbled, slipping out of one shoe, squashing it beneath her foot as the instinct to survive kicked in and gave her the strength to run. The laughter grew louder, zoomed up behind her.

"—until they can get a closer, I don't think any pitcher is going to save—"

The baseball fans.

"Help! Help me!" Brooke glanced desperately around, spotting two uniformed officers walking up the center ramp.

"Brooke!"

Don't listen! Don't look!

The concrete was ice-cold beneath her stockinged foot, the fear charging through her veins even more chilling. She changed direction and ran straight toward the two cops. "Someone's following me. There's a man back there."

"Ma'am?"

"Whoa."

One officer's hand went to his nightstick. He braced and stepped back. *Crazy lady approaching.* The other officer had a quicker sense of her distress. "I don't see any—"

Brooke gestured wildly behind her. "He's been after

me for two days now. I've had flowers and notes and there's laughing. He's always watching. I heard footsteps and saw… there were two trucks—"

"Okay, ma'am. Slow down." The taller of the two officers patted the air, urging her to calm down and make sense. The one with the nightstick searched the garage behind her.

She swallowed hard, tried to catch her breath, but the words erupted again. "There was a man…in the shadows. He was right behind me."

"Brooke?"

That voice was urgent. Familiar. "Atticus?"

"Did I hear you call for help? What's wrong?" She turned to see him jog up behind her. Tall. Imposing. Scowling. She walked straight into his chest, knocking him back half a step before he braced them both. She locked her arms around his waist and grabbed up fistfuls of his jacket as she buried her face at the juncture where his neck met his shoulder.

"O-kay." There was the slightest of hesitation in that word, and in the stiff way he held himself. Then his chest expanded with a deep breath and his arms folded around her. One palm came up beneath the bun at the nape of her neck, gently soothing the tension there. "Okay," he murmured, more affirmation than bewilderment this time. His voice resonated beneath her ear as he spoke over the crown of her head. "Officers, what's the problem?"

"I'm not sure," one answered. "Sounded like she thought someone was after her. Sometimes the vagrants can get in here."

"No." She whispered the certainty against the steady beat of Atticus's heart. "It was him."

"Him?" He must have signaled something to the officers. "I've got this covered. Why don't you take a sweep around and make sure nobody's here who shouldn't be."

"Yes, sir."

"Is she all right?"

"She'll be fine." His hand continued its patient massage. "Right?"

In answer, Brooke squeezed her eyes shut and burrowed impossibly closer. How could one man be so warm? How could one place feel so safe? Her breathing calmed, her pulse no longer thundered in her ears. But she wasn't budging. For the first time in two days, she felt normal again. She hadn't been singled out to be watched or toyed with. She wasn't afraid. She was just…a woman.

A woman whose senses prickled to life as she became aware of so much more than the strength and security Atticus had offered—or rather, that she had helped herself to and he hadn't denied. He was hard in places that she was soft—muscled through the chest and arms, growing leaner down to his waist. He smelled enticingly male. His tie was soft silk, his suit crisp gabardine—well, maybe not so crisp now that she eased her grip on the back of his jacket. His touch was no-nonsense, confident, firm.

He was a lot like the streamlined, not-to-be-messed-with gun her elbow kept bumping at his belt. Protective. Deadly. Steel.

The fanciful metaphor receded to the back of her mind as Atticus leaned back, easing some space between them. He stroked her jaw with the backs of his fingers. "Better?"

She leaned into the caress without thinking, almost purring her positive response. It felt so good to be touched like that.

Opening her eyes, she tilted them up, surprised at how clearly she could see him over the top of her glasses at this short distance. The kaleidoscope of grays in his eyes—silver and dove, pearl and smoke—trapped her, entranced her. Despite the cool colors, they flickered with heat. That heat seemed to move closer. Or maybe she was the one moving, drawn to the flames there.

He cupped her jaw in his hand, nudging her glasses into place with his thumb and blurring his beautiful eyes out of focus. "Brooke?"

Reality check. Atticus was letting go. And if she had any pride or self-sufficiency left in her at all, she'd summon her strength and step away herself.

"Here." Brooke brushed her hair off her face and tucked the loose curls back into her bun as Atticus held up her scraped leather pump. "You threw a shoe back there."

He was trying to make her laugh, gently reminding her that their relationship was of the brother/sister/good friend variety, and that anything extraordinary about heat or eyes or holding tight was all in her imagination. She did smile as she reached for the shoe, though she had an unsettling feeling that her longtime crush on the man had just blossomed into something that could never go back to sisterly again.

She held on to the arm he offered for balance as she lifted one leg and bent down to put the shoe back on. But she quickly released him so he wouldn't feel awkward about her taking advantage again. "Sorry I freaked out on you. I didn't realize it was you calling my name."

There was more cop than man standing before her now, and even her apology couldn't coax his customary smile to return. "You were already running when I stepped off the elevator. It wasn't me who spooked you." He pulled the letter that she'd thrown away from his jacket and held it up to let her know he'd seen the creepy message, too. "I found this in your office, along with a man going through your desk. Does any of that have to do with why you 'freaked out' just now?"

"You went through my trash?"

"Answer my question."

She pressed her lips together and dropped her gaze to the oil-stained concrete before she looked up into his discerning eyes. "Will you walk me to my car?"

"Absolutely."

His hand settled lightly at the back of her waist as they went back up the ramp and headed toward the back of the garage. Brooke tried not to let the politely protective touch distract her, but it was hard to organize her thoughts and express herself rationally when the temptation was there to simply turn into Atticus's body and feel his shielding warmth all through her again.

He traded salutes with the two officers who reported back that they'd seen nothing or no one out of the ordinary on the third level. They'd search the rest of the garage and if anything suspicious turned up, they'd call it in.

They reached her car and he moved ahead to thoroughly check all around, under and inside her VW and the larger vehicles on either side of it before motioning her over and taking the keys to unlock the door for her. But she wasn't getting in. He turned and leaned against the door, bringing his face several inches closer to hers. "Now. Tell me what's going on."

"I guess I let my imagination get away from me."

"Wrong answer." He glanced back the way they'd come, then nailed her with that steely gaze. "You don't have to sugar-coat anything with me. You have an ex-con working for you who conveniently and mysteriously doesn't seem to have any past before he went to prison."

"We're back to Tony, huh?"

"I find a stranger making himself at home in your office, someone's giving you gifts you clearly don't want," he waved the letter in his fist, "you're getting crap like this in the mail—"

"Who was in my office—?"

"And now you think someone's following you? I'm not real comfortable with that much coincidence. I don't care how shy you are, you are going to talk to me."

Atticus Kincaid in his reserved intellectual mode was intimidating enough. Atticus Kincaid determined to have his way was downright scary. Brooke hugged her arms around her middle, feeling a little like a specimen under a microscope.

"Who was in my office?" The question was barely a whisper this time. But the words came out, soft yet clear.

Her insistence on being heard seemed to surprise him as much as her charging into his arms a few minutes ago had. His chest expanded as though he had another argument to make, but then his breath seeped out and he slowly relaxed. A little. "The guy said his name was Mirza Patel. I went to find you after work—I was hoping we'd get a chance to talk about the journal again. He said he left some equipment behind, but I'm pretty sure he was searching through your desk."

"Mirza is a friend from the assertiveness-training class

your dad urged me to take." Another sentence out without a nervous hitch. Nurtured by Atticus's surprising patience, a seed of confidence took root inside her and started to grow. "I worked with him all afternoon, so it's possible he left something behind. I didn't see anything, though. And I don't know why he'd be in my desk. I think…"

Her confidence faltered a bit. This hushed, coherent conversation with Atticus was a new experience for her.

He brushed his finger across her chin and touched his thumb to her bottom lip, gently stopping the self-conscious urge to squeeze her mouth tight. "You think what?"

Brooke's skin heated beneath the contact.

"I think he may like me?" She reached up to adjust her glasses—another nervous habit—and pull away before she read anything more into the intimate gesture than friendly persuasion. "Is that possible?"

"Yeah. It's possible." His gaze swept out to the side and back, the second time she'd seen him do that. Was he expecting her spook from the shadows to show himself? "Do you like him?"

Brooke knew a strangely compelling need to laugh. More nerves? "No. He's a sweet enough friend, but he's not my type. I mean, he is exactly *my* type. We're just alike. Either too stuck in our heads overanalyzing things to speak, or letting it out all at once so we don't make any sense. I mean, can you imagine a conversation between two people like me?"

Atticus stood up straight, reached for her hand and gave it a squeeze after dropping her keys inside. Standing so close to him forced her to tilt her head back to see the bemused grin on his face. "As far as I'm concerned, you're acing Conversation 101 right now. Don't knock what you can do until you try. And keep trying 'til you get it right."

"Thanks for the words of encouragement, oh wise one."

His answering grin was fleeting. He pulled back the front of his jacket and splayed his fingers at his waist, bringing attention to the badge and gun he wore and reminding her that Atticus was a detective first and serving as her life coach was way down on his roles-to-play list. "Though I think stalking the woman you've got the hots for stinks as a seduction strategy, is it possible Patel sent you the flowers and note?"

Brooke shook her head. "I considered that—that maybe he was too shy to say anything. But when I challenged him on it, he reacted more like he wished he'd thought of it rather than being embarrassed or surprised. I don't think Mirza would do that to me."

"Then that puts Fierro back at the top of my list."

"Tony was a thief, not a predator."

Atticus's skepticism was clear on that count. "Don't drop your guard around him for one second. Not until I can find out more about him. Promise me that much, okay? And I don't want you walking out here by yourself again, understand? Ask an officer to escort you. Or call me."

"Okay."

"I mean it, Brooke. How would I explain it to my dad if something happens to you?"

She laughed. Breaking the tension between them felt almost as good as Atticus holding her had. Almost.

He opened the car door for her. It was reassuring to see the smile on his face again. "Get in, already."

After she climbed in, he closed the door and stepped back. But almost as soon as she started the engine, he came back and knocked on her window. Brooke quickly rolled it down. "What is it?"

He braced his arm on the roof of the car and leaned in. "You have a hot date tonight?"

"Me?" Oh, Lordy. Was that a snort? She covered her mouth and cleared her throat. "No. I was just heading home. It's been a long day."

"Too long to go get something to eat with me?"

"I've already wrinkled your jacket, nearly knocked you down and taken up way too much of your time."

"Being with you is never a waste of my time. That's what friends do." She hadn't been thinking of him as a friend recently. In fact, he'd seemed very much like that hero on the white charger when he'd shown up with her shoe and his warmth and attitude. "We never did get around to that journal. So what do you say?"

She'd like to say she'd had more romantic invitations. But then, she had a hard time remembering any invitation recently. And he wasn't really asking her out on a date. He was asking her to work.

"I didn't hear a no." He stooped down to her level and looked her straight in the eye. "So is that a yes?"

What the hell. *Alone* hadn't been working out for her too well the past couple of days. And she truly did want to bring John's killer to justice. If she could be any help at all…

"Do you know where Pearl's Diner is up by the City Market?" Brooke nodded. "I'll buy you a burger and fries."

"Let me call Peggy and Lou to tell them I'll be late. Then I'll meet you there."

"How about I wait right here while you call, and then I'll follow you there."

Yeah. She'd feel safer with Atticus close by. She'd like that. A lot.

She pulled out her phone and dialed their home number. And while she put it to her ear and waited for Peggy or Lou to answer, Brooke reached out and touched one of the extra creases she'd put on the front of Atticus's jacket. "If you want, I can take that to the cleaners and have it pressed for you."

"I've survived worse from you." He turned his hand and laced his fingers through hers. "Make your call."

Chapter Seven

"I swear, I didn't know they were going to be here," Atticus apologized over the half-eaten burgers and fries on the tabletop between them.

"It's okay." Tucked away in the corner of a new booth at Pearl's Diner, sharing her seat with Sawyer and his soon-to-be adopted son, Benjamin, Brooke was a quiet anchor in the chaotic storm that was his family—especially when they were in celebration mode as they were tonight. The news that Sawyer and his wife Melissa were expecting their first child together merited ice cream sundaes with Holden, their mother Susan, and family friend Bill Caldwell.

"Is it as long as me?" Sticky four-year-old fingers tugged at one of the corkscrew curls hanging over Brooke's cheek. Benjamin was a curious little tike who'd developed such a fascination for Brooke's golden-caramel hair that he'd climbed up on the bench seat beside her to play with it. He laughed when he released the tendril and it sprang back into place.

Brooke laughed, too. "Here. Let me help you."

Much better. Pale and frightened was not a look Atticus wanted to see on Brooke's face ever again.

Sitting across from her while everyone chatted around them, his analytical brain couldn't help but compare Brooke's slightly tilted, dimple-to-dimple smile to Hayley's perfectly sculpted lips. There was no comparison.

He'd take *interesting. Real. Honest* over *perfect* any day. Brooke had lips a man could touch without thinking twice about smearing makeup or playing games. He *had* touched them. Hell, he'd almost leaned down and kissed them back there in that parking garage.

Must have been the big green eyes staring up at him over the top of her glasses. Wanting him. Welcoming him. Any man with blood pumping through his veins would have been tempted by such an innocent yet blatant invitation. The desire to kiss Brooke Hansford must have been an extension of the comfort and shelter he'd offered her. Nothing more.

Right. That's why he tuned out his mother, brothers, new sister-in-law and Dutch uncle while they debated family names and new possibilities for the baby, and stared across the table with the same rapt attention as his nephew. Brooke removed a clip and a rubber band, and sent her thick hair tumbling down around her shoulders. A blue-and-white vinyl booth was hardly the setting for a seduction scene, but there was something sensuous about the dramatic fall of hair that made him reconsider the notion that Brooke wasn't an attractive woman. Maybe not conventionally so.

She didn't wear a lot of makeup or terribly flattering clothes, so she wouldn't turn heads when she entered a room. But there were elements of remarkable beauty about her that awakened something a tad territorial inside him. *He'd* noticed those things about Brooke—the eyes, the crooked mouth, those gorgeous, uncoordinated legs. They were *his* secret treasures, *his* discoveries.

The creep with the laugh and the roses who was playing this game of psychological terror with her didn't deserve any part of the hidden treasure that was Brooke. And whether her stalker turned out to be Tony Fierro or some other bastard, he would have Atticus Kincaid to deal with.

"Now pull it straight." Brooke guided a curl into Benjamin's hand. Atticus watched, too, as Ben tugged it behind her back, maybe a little too hard as Brooke winced. But, like a trouper, she didn't complain. "My hair was even longer until a couple of weeks ago."

"Wow. My hair only goes to here." He pulled his black hair down to his eyebrows, then seemed disappointed when it didn't spring back the way hers had. Bored with that bit of research, Ben moved on to the next thing that caught his eye. He climbed onto Sawyer's lap and dug into his shirt pocket. "I wanna give Brooke a cigar."

"Oh, no, Ben, I don't smoke."

Sawyer scooped the boy into his arms and swept him away from the rolled tobacco that he'd handed out to the men around the table. "Don't worry, kiddo, we have special cigars for Big Ben and his friends." Avoiding Ben's grabby hands, Sawyer pulled two cigars—one pink, one blue—from another pocket. "Here, give this one to Brooke."

Sure of Sawyer's grip, Ben simply leaned backward over Sawyer's arm and handed a bubble-gum cigar to Brooke. "I'm gonna have a baby sister or baby bwother."

Brooke accepted the gift. "So I hear. Congratulations."

"Uncle At'kis." Ben swung across to Atticus's side of the table and handed him the other bubble-gum cigar. "You, too."

"Thanks."

Sawyer's petite wife stood up from her chair at the end of the table and announced it was time to go. "One of us has to come back here and work the breakfast shift, so we need to go home and get to bed."

"I like the sound of that." Sawyer winked and Melissa swatted his arm.

"Sawyer! Your mother is sitting right here."

Susan Kincaid sipped the last of her root-beer float and smiled. "Don't mind me. I know where grandchildren come from."

All of the Kincaids laughed. It signaled the end of the festivities. Chairs were returned to their original tables, purses were gathered. There were hugs and handshakes and goodbyes.

Atticus scooted off the bench seat after his mother and rose to kiss Melissa's cheek. "I'm glad you and Pearl got the diner open again so quickly." He was even more glad she'd survived the explosion that her late ex-husband had set in his obsessive need to either own her or destroy her. "Pearl was smart to make you a co-owner. The food's still just as good, but I like the changes I'm seeing."

Melissa nodded her thanks. "There are still a few repairs to be made. But it's mostly exterior work now—finishing the brickwork, painting the sign on the new window. Our regular customers were starting to line up at the door in the mornings, so we had to open up."

Atticus was marginally aware of Brooke remaining in

her seat. But she gave Sawyer a hug, and exchanged words with everyone, so she wasn't completely left out.

"Don't be a stranger." Susan Kincaid squeezed her hand and Brooke smiled.

"I won't."

"All right, let's get this show on the road." Susan directed her sons and extended family toward the front door with the authority of a traffic cop. "Atticus and Brooke came here for a business meeting, and we've gotten them completely off schedule."

Sawyer and Mel went on out to their truck to load Ben into his car seat. While Bill and Holden argued over who was paying the bill, Atticus willingly followed when his mother pulled him aside. She loosened his tie and unbuttoned his collar, worried, as usual, that he was working too much. "Is anything wrong with Brooke? I thought she looked a bit pale when we came in."

Atticus grinned. "You don't think the shock of seeing all of you walk through the door together could turn anyone into a ghost?"

But his mother was too intuitive about such things to laugh. "You're unusually quiet yourself tonight. Now you are certainly not the most rambunctious of my sons, but when I can hear you thinking over in the corner instead of trading zingers with your brothers, I worry."

"I'm okay, Mom."

"And Brooke?"

He wasn't about to lie to his mother, but he wasn't ready to share details about Brooke's unwanted fan or that out-of-place attraction he was feeling for her, either. And he definitely didn't want to get his mother's hopes up about

Brooke's journal and the messages John Kincaid had hidden there.

He opted for a vague version of the truth. "There was an incident on her way home from work, and Brooke was a little rattled by it."

"An incident, hmm?" Susan's warm brown eyes narrowed, telling him she knew there was more to that answer. But she didn't push. Instead, she stretched up on tiptoe to kiss him and hug him tight around the neck. "When you've got it all sorted out in your head, call me, okay? All I want to do is listen. In the meantime, you look out for her. Brooke means too much to this family to allow her to be hurt."

"I'm looking out for her, Mom. And I'll call soon, I promise."

Susan smiled and cupped his cheek. "Look out for yourself, too."

"Su, are you ready?" Bill Caldwell walked up behind Susan. He extended his hand to Atticus. "Good to see you again, A."

"You, too," Atticus replied, shaking hands.

"Making any progress?"

Susan gave him a reproving look. "Bill, you promised we wouldn't talk about John's murder. We're celebrating Sawyer and Melissa's news tonight."

Caldwell's eyes crinkled in a wry frown beside the silver streaks at his temples. "I'm sorry, Su. I don't mean to spoil the evening." He draped his arm around her shoulders and gave her an apologetic squeeze. His arm settled comfortably in place and remained there. "But a man starts to get a little paranoid when not one, but two of his friends are murdered. James McBride served with John and me in the army before he came to work for me at Caldwell Technologies. I keep going over names of anyone the two of them would be connected to, including me. There were other men from that same unit whom I've hired over the years, either full-time or as consultants. Do I tell them they may be on some hit list, too?"

The hackles at the back of Atticus's neck went up when he saw the stricken look on his mother's face. "Drop it, Bill."

"I'm ashamed to admit that I'm a little afraid myself." It seemed to require a monumental amount of will for Caldwell to first make the admission, and then set it aside. A man who ran a multimillion-dollar technology development corporation probably wasn't used to being unable to control of every facet of his life. "My offer to post a reward for information still stands. Any amount, you name it. Or I can hire a team of private investigators if that will help."

"KCPD will find Dad's killer," Atticus insisted. When they lost one of their own, they took care of it. That was probably why he was willing to risk his career by poking through Brooke's journal before letting Detective Grove decide whether or not there was any useful information in it.

He'd lost one of his own.

Caldwell nodded. "Of course. I have every faith that you and your brothers will get the job done. Look at the man who raised you."

"Aww, Bill." Susan reached up to pat Bill's hand where it still rested on her shoulder. And if those were tears that suddenly glistened in her eyes, she quickly wiped them away. "My sons are the best legacy John could have possibly left behind."

"All right, already. So I'm a god. All this mushiness has to stop." Sometime during the conversation, Holden had joined their circle. His tongue-in-cheek humor was just the ticket to elicit a laugh from Susan, which eased Atticus's concern as well. With the mood of the group officially lifted, Holden leaned over and kissed the top of her head. "I'll drive you home, Mom."

Bill Caldwell waved the offer aside. "I brought your mom. I can take her home."

Susan Kincaid wrapped her arm around the waist of her youngest son and tilted her head back to see his face. "Thanks, hon. But your apartment's in a different direction and I know you've come off your two-day shift and need some sleep. I'll just ride with Bill."

"I don't mind."

She pulled him down to her level for a hug and kissed him. "Go home."

She tapped Atticus in the middle of the chest and slyly pointed toward the booth where he'd left Brooke sitting by herself. "Go back before she thinks you've abandoned her."

He nodded.

"And Atticus?" He watched her expression change from teasing to solemn. "Brooke always took such good care of your father. You take good care of her."

"I will."

Atticus held the door open for his mother and Bill, but Holden stayed put, waiting until the glass door swung shut again before speaking.

He nodded toward Caldwell and their mother as the older gentleman helped her into his Mercedes. "You okay with that?"

"I trust Bill to drive her home."

Holden's blue eyes reflected his concern. "Don't be so dense, smart guy. I mean the fact that he's hittin' on Mom. Hell, it's only been three months since we buried Dad."

"Bill? He was Dad's best friend. One of Mom's, too. They're leaning on each other for support right now because they're both still in mourning."

"If you say so. They've been spending a lot of time together lately. And he keeps finding reasons to touch her."

Old friends becoming lovers? Maybe the idea of such a change was a little unsettling. But Atticus wasn't sure he was thinking of his mother and Bill Caldwell.

No. Finding his father's killer came first. Doing his job came first. Preserving a perfectly good relationship as it was would be the smart thing to do. "I wouldn't worry too much. Mom isn't ready to start seeing anyone yet."

"Maybe. But does *he* know that?" They stood and watched until Bill Caldwell and their mother drove away. But instead of heading out the door himself, Holden hooked his thumbs into the back pockets of his jeans and made himself at home in Atticus's business. "And what's the deal with you and Brooke? You've been sneakin' looks at her all night long."

Atticus let his gaze slide over to the table. Brooke didn't even seem to notice that she was alone. She'd already opened up the journal and was poring over it, nearly nose to page, as she read through it without her glasses. Wearing them perched on top of her head, there was something adorably earnest yet vulnerable about the utter concentration lining her eyes.

"Yeah, A. Sneakin' looks just like that one." Man, that was a wicked grin.

"There is no *deal*." He thumped Holden on the shoulder, telling him he was making more out of a couple of glances and attentive old friends than he needed to. "What Mom said. Go home."

Ignoring the teasing overtones of Holden's laugh, Atticus pushed him out the door and returned to his ice-cold dinner. "Hey. You want to try again? We can order something hot to eat."

"No, thanks." Her lip disappeared as her gaze darted to the window. But she never looked at him.

Sliding back into the seat across from Brooke, Atticus briefly wondered if there was any merit to what Holden had said. Could Bill be developing more than a friendly interest in Susan Kincaid? Was there a parallelism to his own observations of Brooke?

And what the heck was she up to now?

Climbing up on her knees in the vinyl seat, she pulled her glasses back into place and peered out the diner's front window to the sidewalk below. She glanced down at the journal, then back to the sidewalk. Curious.

"Brooke?"

"It's a brick!"

"Excuse me?"

She pointed out the window. "The pallets out there gave me the idea. Well, it's a rock. I don't actually have bricks. But I had talked about changing the interior with your father at one time. In the end, Peggy and Lou and I decided to stick with the limestone to be consistent with—"

He tried to slow her down. "What are you talking about?"

"The map in the journal." She cleared a spot on the table and spun the book around, pointing to the markings

on the picture. "B6N. Brick 6 North. NR. New Row."
Before he could focus in, she closed the book and stuffed
it into her purse, uncurling her legs and moving out of the
booth all at the same time. "When Mr. McCarthy and his
men installed the double door leading to the sun porch, they
had to add an extra row of new limestone blocks because
the original 1896 archway was too high to fit modern
standard door measurements. John was there the day they
were refitting the archway. He's talking about the bricks."
Her fingers skittered in the air as she tried to halt her own
rapid gunfire ramblings. "I mean the blocks."

"Why?"

"I don't know." She was on her feet now, pulling her skirt
back down around her calves and slinging her purse up over
her shoulder. "But I intend to locate B6N and find out."

"Whoa, whoa." He grabbed her arm as she scooted past.
"Where are you going?"

"Home." She tugged against his grip, inviting him to
join her, not pulling away. "Are you coming with me?"

Oh, yeah. Her brain was cookin'. Her excitement was
contagious. He tossed a couple of bills onto the table, and
hurried to join her on her way out the door.

Chapter Eight

"The scenes with all the snow should cool you off just fine."

Brooke set the note on the granite counter and smiled. Normally, she would have loved to check out a classic movie like *Dr. Zhivago* with her aunts. But tonight she was a woman on a mission. It was about to get noisy and dusty in here, and it would probably send Louise into some kind of conniption to see any of the carefully reconstructed church being torn apart again. Tonight, she was glad to have the house to herself.

Well, mostly to herself.

"The note from Aunt Peggy says they decided to drive over to Glenwood to see *Dr. Zhivago* at the Retro. After working outside for most of the day, they thought an air-conditioned theater was the best way to beat the summer heat." She spread her arms in a wide gesture and apologized for the house's muggy atmosphere. "As you can tell, we don't have the central air running yet."

"Not a problem."

Not for her, at any rate. Atticus Kincaid was dangerous sophistication in his suit and tie. But tonight he'd shed the jacket and rolled up his sleeves to set up two ladders and scaffolding in front of the locked double doors leading to her unfinished sunporch. The air of danger still clung to him as she watched him work. She supposed the holster he wore and his get-the-job-done focus added that. But there was something more earthy, more intimate about exposing the tanned column of his throat and the dusting of dark hair along his forearms as his muscles flexed with the task and glistened in response to the heat of the summer night.

The heavy toolbox she'd carried out to the kitchen from her bedroom rattled like Jacob Marley's chains when she picked it up and hauled it over to the sunporch doors. "I'll go ahead and open some windows. If there's any breeze at all, we'll get a decent crosscurrent."

"Here." He hopped down from the three-foot platform he'd built and took the toolbox from her grip. What she'd toted with two hands, he picked up in a smooth one-handed swing and set it on the scaffolding. "We'll need a hammer and chisel to break up that mortar, and then a pry bar to move those rocks."

Perhaps succumbing a bit to the heat herself, Brooke unhooked the top two buttons of her blouse as she watched him sort through the tools and pull on a pair of canvas work gloves. His back and shoulders flexed with each precise movement and she wondered how shameless it would seem if she kept right on unhooking buttons.

The windows. *Open the windows and cool off before you embarrass yourself.* Not that she was any kind of expert in the art of catching a man's eye, but she had a feeling that drooling would not be the most attractive thing she could do. "I'll just get the windows," she said out loud, needing the extra impetus to move away from him.

Atticus was diving into this treasure hunt with as much enthusiasm as she. He trusted that her idea was the right one—at least it was good enough for him to take a chance on. She didn't know which it was that made her nerves dance and her skin flush with anticipation—working beside the sexy detective or basking in his unqualified support of her crazy idea.

Staying true to its architectural design, they'd left the shape of the original church windows intact—tall and narrow, running from thigh height to near the line of the ceiling. And though each window came to a point with stained-glass inserts at the top, the bottom of each window had been fitted with modern insulated frames with shades installed between the glass.

"You lock those at night, right?" Atticus queried. "At that height, especially, I can't tell you how easy it'd be to cut the screen and climb in if someone wanted to."

She pushed the first window open, deciding this wasn't the time to admit that she and her aunts did sleep with their bedroom windows open at night. It was just too darn hot not to. "We plan to have a security system installed before the construction is completed."

Meaning it wasn't there now. Meaning she didn't have to admit anything—Atticus already knew. She felt his heat behind her a split second before he reached around to inspect the window's new locks for himself. "Lock them when it's just you or your aunts here," he ordered. "It's better to sweat than to scream. Remember how you felt in that parking garage this afternoon?"

Helpless. Terrified.

She shivered at the ominous words of wisdom. A second

later, his gloved hands were on her shoulders, kneading away the fear, kindling a whole new different kind of tension.

"I'm not trying to scare you," he whispered against her ear. His breath danced along her neck. His touch warmed her deep inside. Atticus's massage felt completely different from Mirza's awkward grope. This touch felt seductive. Intimate. Right. "I just want you to be smart. And safe."

Brooke nodded. "I will."

Before she succumbed to the urge to lean into his sheltering body once more, he pulled away and returned to work. "So all that lumber stacked outside is to finish the second floor and sundeck?"

"That's right."

"And the flagstones?"

She opened another window and followed him back to the scaffolding. "Paving the sunporch."

He set the toolbox on the floor and climbed to the three-foot platform. "It looks like McCarthy has more supplies and equipment outside than you have room for in here."

"We gutted everything from floor to ceiling, so there's been plenty to rebuild inside."

"Plenty of places out there for a man to hide if he wanted to."

Brooke looked up at his stern countenance, towering above her. A shadow of evening beard stubble only seemed to darken his expression. "You know, as far as giving reassuring pep talks go, you suck."

His chest-deep laugh took years off his tight-lipped expression and dissipated the dire mood his matter-of-fact warnings had created. "If you want warm fuzzies, talk to Sawyer. If you want the facts, I'm your man." With a mockingly gallant bow, he held out his hand to help her climb up. "May I?"

Kicking off the beat-up heels she still wore, Brooke wrapped her fingers around the worn canvas glove and strong hand underneath. Warm fuzzies were fine for a big brother. Atticus's unvarnished facts and abundant skills and strengths made her feel safe, yet off-kilter in a way that was as unfamiliar as it was exciting.

Once she stood beside him, he picked up the hammer and chisel. "So where do I start?"

The new row of stones and mortar above the door frame was obvious. Brooke studied the puzzle. "I don't know if your dad meant to count six blocks *to* the north, or to count *from* the north end."

Atticus handed her a pair of safety goggles like the ones he'd put on, and counted off the limestone blocks with the chisel. "Looks like the second one from either end. Where do you want me to do the damage?"

Brooke reviewed the design of John's sketch in her mind and decided. "This one."

Like forensic archaeologists, Atticus hammered and chipped away at the mortar while Brooke brushed away the dust and concrete bits that held the block in place between layers of century-old stone and modern engineering. Anticipation kicked in, exciting her pulse as inch by inch, a little more of the double-shoe-box-sized limestone block was revealed.

"Here." Atticus handed her the tools as the stone began to shift inside the cavity they were opening around it.

Brooke dropped the hammer, chisel and brush in the tool box and quickly returned to assist him. "How heavy is it?"

Dust clung to the perspiration on his arms and forehead, and turned the shoulders of his white shirt to ecru. He glanced down at her outstretched hands. "Too heavy for you to catch. Back up."

Dutifully retreating to the edge of the scaffolding, Brooke twisted her body, mimicking the pushing and tugging of Atticus's arms as he jimmied the stone loose. "And we—" she heard the clunk of the last bit of mortar giving way "—have—" stone grated against stone "—victory!"

"Yes!" Brooke pumped her fists as the rock slid free from the wall.

"Not bad teamwork, eh? Let's clean out the hole and make sure there aren't any little critters or sharp…or, you could just check it out for yourself."

Only momentarily distracted by the bulge of Atticus's muscles as he took the full weight of the stone and set it down, Brooke hurried over to the gaping hole. Bracing one hand against the door frame, she stretched up on tiptoe and stuck her arm inside. Grit. Cool stone. Rough concrete. Her fingertips brushed against something softer, small and bulky, in the back corner. "Oh, my gosh. Oh, my gosh!"

"What?" A strong arm snaked around her waist and pulled her away from the wall.

"Yes!" Brooke twisted, wrapping her arms around Atticus's neck. "We found it!" Between the adrenaline rush and gravity, they teetered over the edge.

"Ah, hell. Hold on." Atticus closed both arms around her and jumped before they fell.

Landing with a jolt she barely felt, Brooke clutched her prize in her hand and kissed the side of his neck. His skin was warm and salty, the stubble of his beard like the finest of sandpaper against her lips.

Still riding the euphoria of solving the mystery of the journal and falling through the air to land quite safely against Atticus's solid, unyielding chest, her senses were already intensified. The kiss, chaste in and of itself, rippled like a shock wave through her system, short-circuiting shyness and sensibilities. She dragged her mouth up along the cordings of his neck until her lips found the sharp line of his jaw and changed directions.

"Yes." She cheered on their success with a throaty whisper. Kissed the point of his chin. "Yes!"

She pressed her lips against his with an instinct so natural that she hardly realized it was a kiss. But something deep inside her knew. Even in her untutored experience she knew she wanted to kiss him again. And again.

Her fingers knew to comb through the trim ebony silk of his hair and guide his mouth to hers. Her body knew to stretch out against him, echoing the friction between his harder mouth and her softer, seeking lips. She took the kiss she wanted. Demanded another. She…

Oh. No.

The adrenaline wore off and reality rushed in, heating her face with embarrassment. Clenching her stomach with regret. Filling her brain with excuses and apologies and the command to run.

In her mindless celebration, she'd literally thrown herself at the man and was kissing the stuffing out of him.

She gave a token swipe to the hair she'd mussed and quickly pulled her hands down. *I'm sorry. My fault.* Get the words out. Make the awkward moment go away.

But when she tried to step back, his hands locked at her waist. "Don't stop now."

Atticus's words were laced with portent, his eyes with promise. Brooke watched in wide-eyed wonder as he leaned in. With his thumb and forefinger he nudged her chin up. Even when he paused to pull off his gloves and toss them, the focus of those steely eyes never wavered away from her mouth.

"My turn," he whispered. His fingertips came back to frame her face, angling it back another fraction of an inch as he closed his mouth over hers.

For a moment, Brooke froze in shock. Atticus Kincaid was kissing her! No, he was embracing her, seducing her. And she was... What was she doing? She'd braced her palms against his chest, neither holding on nor pushing away. She was desperately trying to focus on his expression—through her glasses, beneath her glasses—and read his intent.

"Shh." With the pad of his thumb, he touched the swell of her lower lip, coaxing her mouth to open. She hadn't said a word, hadn't made a noise, and yet the calming sound of his voice, the gentling touch of his hand, seemed to reach out to that turbulent place inside her and turn off that internal chaos. "Relax," he coached. "Let me do this." He smiled against her lips. "And kiss me back. If you want to."

She did.

With a deep sigh that cleared away self-conscious second-guessing, Brooke slid her hands up Atticus's chest and twined them lightly behind his neck. Her mouth opened, her heart expanded, and she melted into him.

"Better." He moved one hand to the center of her back

and pulled her close. The other hand cupped the flare of her hip and aligned them, chest to chest, thigh to thigh. His lips were firm, thorough and achingly patient as he set about exploring each corner and curve of her mouth. "Much better."

As impulsive and instinctual as those first kisses had been, Brooke now analyzed every nuance of movement—the warm rasp of his tongue sliding across her lips, the way the muscles in his chest hitched when she rubbed against him to ease the tingling friction that made her breasts heavy and her nipples hard. She marveled at every visceral response—the desire to touch her tongue to his, the tightening and unfurling deep inside when he squeezed her bottom and lifted her against the swelling desire behind his zipper. She curled her toes behind his knee and tightened her grip around his shoulders, shamelessly pulling herself closer and begging for the next lesson in passion to be taught.

"Atticus. Att—" Squirming against his solid chest and corded thighs, Brooke felt something hot and liquid swirling up inside her. "More." She slid her palms against the tickling silk of his short hair. "I want…" She caught his chin lightly between her teeth, loving the salty taste of his skin as much as she liked the tiny sensations of each prickle of beard stubble abrading her lips. "I've always wanted…"

She thrust her tongue inside his mouth, sampling the softer, hotter skin there, finding the same pleasure he seemed to find when he'd done the same to her. His answering moan, husky and deep in his throat, washed over her like fuel to a flame. He lifted her higher and she was moving, spinning. His hands roamed, squeezed, heated her skin beneath every touch. And then Brooke felt the hard granite counter beneath her bottom. Atticus's hands were a flurry of action, as precise as they were swift. He removed her glasses, sifted her hair across her shoulders, parted her thighs and moved between them as he took command of the kiss and began to teach her skill after skill. A nip, a taste. A harder touch, a softer one.

"Much, much better," he whispered against her lips before claiming them again. He pushed her skirt up past her knees and slid his hands beneath the hem, stroking her all along the length of her thighs. "These are gorgeous, honey. Sexy gorgeous. Don't hide them from me, okay?"

Brooke nodded, unable to speak, barely able to understand. *Sexy? Gorgeous?* Had she ever heard those words applied to her before? She committed to memory every delicious sensation—his distinct male scent, musky with exertion and desire, and the deep-pitched rasp of his voice as he whispered against her mouth.

"This is crazy. Completely irrational. You're Brooke."

"Yes."

"You're *Brooke*," he articulated more succinctly, piercing the fog of desire swirling up inside her. He removed his hands from beneath her skirt and brought them up to frame her face. His chest rose and fell with the same jagged rhythm as her own. He rested his forehead against hers, his silvery eyes dark and drowsy and so close to hers as she tried to make sense of what was happening to her. To them. "We'd better slow this down before your aunts walk in on us."

"Please?" She skimmed her hands along his arms, her sensitized fingers moving over crisp hair and feverish skin and dusty cotton before retracing their path. Though her mind understood the common sense of what he was saying—that this was too fast, too much—that, in a matter of minutes, they might no longer be alone—she also believed that there was something magical here. Something worth the risk. Something just out of reach that they'd nearly discovered together. She clenched her knees around his hips, her body shamelessly asking for something it had been denied.

"Whoa, honey. Brooke. We need to stop." Atticus stiffened his arms and stumbled back a step, blurring out of focus.

Chilling rapidly, fully aware and feeling suddenly self-conscious, Brooke pressed her knees together and hugged her arms across her chest. She fumbled with her collar, tucking her necklace inside and straightening the wrinkled cotton. "I'm sorry." She squinted, struggling to bring the dark-haired blob that was Atticus Kincaid into focus. "I'm not terribly sophisticated about such things, and I know I got carried away. I mean, we were celebrating and then I was—" Oh, Lordy "—climbing…on you. And I—"

"Shh." A finger pressed against her lips as Atticus snapped into focus. "I'm not complaining." He placed her glasses in her hand and as she slipped them on, donning her plain-Jane persona again, he smoothed a trio of stray curls away from her face. "I just wasn't expecting it."

With her glasses on, she could see the perplexity that deepened the grooves beside his eyes and mouth. He did seem truly baffled by the passion that had flared between them.

Good. She didn't want to be the only one trying to figure this out. But was it the passion or the woman he'd nearly lost control with that had him thinking so hard to piece together the clues and find answers?

Atticus clasped her waist and lifted her from the countertop. "You're full of surprises, aren't you?" Brooke was vaguely aware of her toes touching the planked floor. He quickly released her with a comment that was both flattering and unsettling. "I always heard it was the quiet ones a man had to watch out for. But I never realized they were talking about you."

"I'm a bit of a danger to you, aren't I?" She worried her bottom lip with her tongue, surprised to feel it slightly swollen, but even more surprised to see the way his gaze darted to the self-conscious movement. "Did I hurt anything when I knocked us off the platform? I got a little excited."

"I got a little carried away, too." Easing a bit more space between them, he smoothed her hair away from her face, framing her jaw and touching his thumb to her sensitized lip. "Don't worry. I'm a big boy. I can handle myself okay."

He handled himself—and her—like a pro.

"Now," he plucked a chip from the tangled strands of her loose hair, "let's see what you found, detective."

Still breathless from his kiss and unsure what to say anyway, Brooke simply nodded and opened her hand between them, revealing a dust-coated wad of material. Brooke unwrapped the faded blue cloth until she got to the treasure inside—a tiny red envelope that said Cattlemen's Bank, with the number 333 handwritten in black marker across the back. "A safe deposit key."

"Don't look so disappointed." Atticus unsnapped the envelope and pulled out the thin key inside. "This is standard issue. There must be a dozen branches of the Cattlemen's Bank in the Kansas City area. We should be able to track down a location and get permission to open the box it goes to."

"And then what? Another cryptic clue?" Brooke huffed out a weary sigh, missing the full-body contact and already fretting that that embrace had been a fluke of the moment—something to be treasured but never repeated. Her frustrations spilled over and blended together. "I guess I thought we'd find answers here. Instead, I've torn up my house and wasted your time. I wanted to find a lead on the case for you. And for John."

"You didn't waste anything." He closed his hand around her shoulder and gave her a reassuring squeeze. "You gave me something I haven't had for a long time."

A wrenched back? An amusing story to tell his friends?

"What's that?"

"Hope." He dipped his head, and Brooke actually braced her hand against his chest, thinking he meant to give her one more kiss. But she must have misunderstood his intent because he abruptly pulled away. "Here." He dropped the key into her palm and curled her fingers around it. "You better hold on to this. I could get into serious trouble with Major Taylor if I show up with potential evidence that I haven't cleared through Grove and Homicide first. Now, you want me to help you clean up this mess? Or should I drive back to the office and start tracking down the box that goes with that key?"

Though disappointed by the lost kiss, she smiled, anyway. This was about solving John's murder, not her misreading signals. "What do you think?"

He nodded, moving like a man on a mission as he grabbed his jacket off the back of a stool. "I'll call you as soon as I find out anything. Tomorrow, after the banks are open, we'll check it out."

Drained by the ups and downs of her evening, Brooke led him to the back door. Though he made no mention whatsoever of either kiss, she did like the "we" part of what he was saying. There *was* hope that the key in her hand was something John Kincaid had left behind for her to find. And there was hope that she and Atticus could continue to work together to uncover the truth about John's murder.

The air outside was thick and warm on her face when she opened the door. After sweeping up, a cooling shower and spending a little more time with John's notes sounded like a good plan for the evening.

Atticus hooked his jacket over his shoulder and turned on the deck, urging her back into the house. "Lock this door behind me."

"I will."

"And don't forget to lock the windows."

"Yes, sir."

He reached out, stroked his fingers along her jaw. His lips parted, as though he had more directions he wanted to give her. "Such a surprise," he said instead, before pulling his hand away. "See you in the morning."

With a nod, Brooke locked the door, then fetched the broom and dustpan out of the utility closet and walked over to the scaffolding to start cleaning up. She was just beginning to formulate the story she'd tell her aunts about the hole in the wall when the telephone rang.

Leaning the broom against the platform, Brooke hurried over to the phone on the kitchen counter and answered.

"Hello?" Silence answered. The caller ID didn't show her anything. Wrong number? Disconnected call? "Hello?"

The mood instantly changed as the silence became breathing. And the breathing became two words. "Pretty lady."

Familiar, low-pitched laughter increased in volume, drowning out the fear pounding in her ears.

"You're mine, pretty lady. Don't forget that. You're mine."

Brooke slammed the phone down on its base and ran to her purse to pull out her cell. The heat of the night couldn't penetrate the chill that worked its way into her bones as she found Atticus's number and dialed it.

"Detective Kincaid."

Thank God. Deep. Strong. No-nonsense.

Brooke nearly wept at the sound of his voice. "He was on the phone. Just now. He called."

Atticus didn't ask for details. "I'm on my way."

Brooke shut her phone and hugged her arms tightly around her waist. Should she lock herself in the bathroom until he got here? Turn off the lights so no one could see her inside? Alone?

"Oh, my God." She looked across the main room to the open windows that had seemed so benign less than an hour ago. Hating how exposed and vulnerable she suddenly felt in the soaring dimensions of her own home, Brooke dashed to the windows.

She had barely touched the glass when someone pounded at her back door. Startled by the noise, she screamed.

"Brooke!"

"Atticus? Atticus!" She ran to the door and unlocked it. In one smooth move, he tucked her to his chest, backed her into the kitchen and locked the door behind him. Brooke curled her fingers into the front of his shirt and held on. "How did you get here so fast?"

"I was parked outside, watching the place, waiting for you to lock the damn windows. Are you all right?" He caught her face between his hands and hunched down, looking straight into her eyes, searching hard for answers. "Brooke, are you all right?" he repeated.

When she nodded, he palmed the back of her head and kissed her, firm and fast—some sort of territorial stamp that spoke little of common sense and more of the relief that crowded her thoughts. Switching his grip to her hand, he went to secure the windows and close the shades himself. He kept her right with him as he moved from room to room through the main floor of the house, testing other windows, looking under beds, in closets. He checked the phone and cursed that there was no number, adding that to his list of things to track down tomorrow. Only when he seemed satisfied that all was safe did he sit her on a kitchen stool, pour her a cup of hot coffee and ask her to tell him exactly what happened.

There wasn't much to tell. "He said…" She clutched the warm mug between her hands and swallowed past the lump of fear in her throat. "He said, 'You're mine, pretty lady.' Warned me never to forget that. And he laughed. Like this is some kind of joke to him. Like *I'm* some kind of joke."

"No." Atticus brushed a tendril of hair from her eyes, but she could barely feel his heat or believe his reassurance.

"I don't understand why he wants me to be afraid. I don't understand why he wants me at all."

"Do you have a sleeping bag?"

She nodded, the abrupt switch in topic startling her from her morbid thoughts. "Why?"

"Because you don't have a couch. And I'm staying the night."

Brooke set down her mug and tried to stand. "But my aunts—"

"I am staying the night."

FORTY-FOUR. Forty-five. Antonio turned off his headphones and concentrated on the weights hooked at his ankles.

So the virgin and the cop were gettin' it on. Antonio idly wondered if she'd still be a virgin by morning light.

Nah. Kincaid was too much of a straight-shooter and she was too much of lily-white wimp to go after what she wanted so badly. If she'd begged him like that, he would have taken her.

He might still take her.

The boss could erase the trophies of his past from public record, but they couldn't be erased from *his* memory. Twelve women, all bowing to his will.

But none of them had been a virgin. And Brooke Hansford screamed of waiting-for-that-one-man-to-come-along thing.

Yeah. He should take her.

But business came first.

Savoring the burn in his thighs, he lifted the weight for the last rep. An almost transcendental calm spread through him. He'd finished another workout, and he'd gotten lucky far quicker than even he had anticipated.

Time to report in. He picked up the phone beside the bench and dialed a number that couldn't be traced.

This was all too easy. He held a power over Brooke Hansford now that she couldn't begin to comprehend. And while that kind of advantage over another person stirred powerful urges inside him, he was more pleased about how his employer would reward his success. The boss wouldn't be able to argue his talents or question his loyalty now.

"Yes?"

Antonio didn't bother with a greeting, either. "The bugs I put in place are working."

"I told you they were state-of-the-art."

The implication that setting up the two receivers inside Brooke Hansford's house had more to do with technology than with his covert skills rankled. But he'd gain the boss's respect yet. "She was searching for something tonight. Found it. Sounds like a lock-box key."

"I want it. Take it from her."

Antonio wiped the perspiration from his upper lip. "My pleasure."

Chapter Nine

"When I challenged you to start talking to more men, I didn't realize you'd bring one home to practice with." Louise was practically rubbing her hands together as she watched Brooke work. "It's an interesting enough development that I'm willing to forgive you tearing apart my archway."

Brooke tied off the sleeping bag where Atticus had probably spent a miserable night on the floor of the foyer between the two finished bedrooms and rolled to her feet. Louise trailed right behind her as she carried the bag back to the storage space underneath her antique bed. "Atticus is looking out for me as a favor to his dad, I'm sure. He's here as a police officer, Louise, not to entertain your matchmaking fantasies."

Though as she stooped down to slide the bag beneath the iron bed, she couldn't help but notice how his uniquely male scent clung to the padded cotton. Nothing else in this house smelled that good, and if she paused to inhale an extra sniff, who could blame her?

"I saw that."

"You saw nothing." Brooke popped up and glared at her

single-minded aunt. "I was just noting that I probably should have aired it out before loaning it to him last night. It still smells a bit like mothballs."

Louise grinned. "Oh, honey, you are an atrocious liar. He smells like pure man, and nothing is better than that."

Brooke thought she might collapse from heatstroke as Louise's words hit a self-conscious nerve wired to every cell in her body. She propped her hands at her hips, thankful that Atticus was in the shower across the hall and couldn't hear this embarrassing conversation. "Atticus is a friend," she articulated. "A good one who's willing to sleep on a hard floor without air conditioning because I got that crank call and was a little…out of sorts last night."

Finding that key and getting a crash course in kissing hadn't done much to settle her nerves, either. Had she made a complete fool of herself? Been an amusing aberration for such an obviously experienced man? Did he regret the momentary distraction either because it had diverted his attention from pursuing his father's killer or because he now felt obligated to provide off-the-clock protection for her? Were they supposed to talk about what had happened? How could she figure out what the next step should be when she wasn't even certain she was supposed to take one?

But Louise wanted what Louise wanted. "So he smells good and he's chivalrous, to boot. You ought to reel that one in."

"I don't know how—" She put up her hand, warding off both her aunt's well-intentioned scheming and her own debilitating fluster. "No. No. I won't let you do this to me. Atticus and I are working together on an investigation. He believes his father left me some information about whatever trouble he was in that may have gotten him killed. He hid it in my things probably because I'm so easy to overlook that no one would suspect—"

"You are *not* easy to overlook." Louise stamped her foot, defending the niece she loved to the same degree that she drove her nuts. "Not to anyone with any sense. If Mr. Kincaid did leave you a hidden message, it was because he knew he could count on you to figure it out. And he knew that big heart of yours would help him—and his sons—come hell or high water."

Eccentricities aside, Brooke loved her aunt, and would be forever grateful that even though she'd been denied her birth parents, she'd been given to two wonderful women to become a part of their family. "You know, Aunt Lou, you make it impossible to stay mad at you."

"I know." Louise turned to the open door of Brooke's closet. "Now. What are you going to wear today?"

"I'm dressed."

In that? Louise didn't have to say the words. She started sorting through each hanger. "I think something with a shorter hemline."

Brooke groaned. Maybe not completely impossible.

BROOKE WONDERED if it was a fortunate or scary thing that she could fit into Louise's clingy navy wraparound silk skirt. The celadon-green blouse was her own, but Louise had insisted on leaving two buttons unhooked at the top. Brooke wasn't budging on the bun and wearing her hair down, not with nearly hundred-degree temperatures expected by the end of this afternoon. And she wasn't wearing the bright-red lipstick, either.

Baby steps, Aunt Peggy had warned, when she came in to see why it was taking so long to come to breakfast. Atticus had already finished his pancakes and bacon, and advised her on simple security precautions they should take, from letting any call their caller *ID* didn't recognize go straight to the answering machine, to establishing a neighborhood watch, to the bit about the windows again. "If I offer him anything more to eat, he's going to think I'm trying to fatten him up. Now quit your fiddling, and let the girl get going. He said he wants to leave by seven-thirty so he'll have time to get into the city and change his clothes before he has to report for duty."

"Let's try dangly earrings." Louise opened another drawer of her jewelry cabinet. "They're sexy."

Peggy took Brooke by the hand and pulled her away from the mirror where Louise was concocting her transformation. "Detective Kincaid has been on the phone to KCPD twice already this morning, and he's gone over every lock on this house with a fine-tooth comb. He appreciates hard work and punctuality. He won't be swayed by a pair of your dangly earrings."

"Thanks for the rescue," Brooke whispered to Peggy on their way out the door.

"Are you kidding?" Peggy wasn't above a little fairy godmothering herself as she straightened Brooke's collar. "He's not here to spend time with me and my home cooking. Now get out there."

Traitor.

Brooke's mouth was still gaping open when she entered the kitchen area and found Atticus sitting at the island counter, poring over her journal. A quick scan last night had assured her that the personal contents were limited to career aspirations and future goals—nothing as potentially humiliating as the rambling thoughts she'd recorded last night in another volume. They'd included a few brief paragraphs along the lines of how a woman could know the difference between making a colossal mistake and pushing for what she wanted with a man. That one, she thought thankfully, would never see eyes other than her own. Still, it was a bit disconcerting to see something so private being dissected and notated in the small notebook Atticus normally carried in his pocket.

Some sixth sense, or her own lack of stealth, must have alerted him to her presence. He glanced up from his notes. "Good morning."

He looked surprisingly well-rested, not at all perturbed by events from the night before, the rat. And though his clothes were still creased and dusty from the adventures she'd put him through yesterday, he was clean-shaven and his short hair glistened like spikes of polished obsidian from the dampness of his shower.

She had to snap her jaw shut before she could answer. "I see you found the disposable razor I set out."

Ah, yes. That was clever repartee.

"I don't know that pink is my color, but it got the job done. Thanks."

"No problem." With her aunts conspicuously absent, Brooke had a hard time coming up with what to say next. *How did you sleep?* Trite. A hard floor was a hard floor. *Will there be any more kissing lessons today?* Too desperate. Perfect setup for laughter of some kind.

Work should be a safe enough topic. She nodded toward the journal. "Did you find anything useful?"

"I'm copying down everything Dad wrote. Some of it is really out of context, like this bit about tracing genealogy in Germany. The Kincaids are as Irish as they come. Or maybe this has to do with you." He eyed her over the top of his reading glasses. "Your ancestry isn't German, is it?"

"Not that I know of." A spark of an idea tried to show itself. "This is a German church. The settlers who built it were from Bingen. I don't know why your dad would comment on that, though."

"Me, either. And there are so many abbreviations, it's hard to see any kind of pattern." He removed his reading glasses and closed the journal. "Maybe you can make sense of it for me later."

"I'll try."

He slipped his notebook inside his jacket pocket. "Will it still work to drive you into the city? Or would you prefer that I follow you in your car?"

"Since we're running to the bank at lunch, we can just go together this morning. If you're sure you don't mind driving me home again. That seems like a big imposition."

"It's not," he answered matter-of-factly, folding his glasses and putting them away.

"Are you sure? Because I could call a cab, too. Or have Peggy pick me up when she's out to the grocery store. Or maybe we should drive separately, after all."

"It's no imposition. Especially since I'll be spending the night here again, anyway."

"You…? Again…?"

"You can't talk me out of it," he stated, as if she'd just offered up a logical argument instead of babbling her surprise. "Even if I have to sleep outside in my car for propriety's sake with your aunts—" heck, no, they'd have him sleeping in her room if they could manage it "—I am not leaving you unprotected. You're the key to understanding whatever Dad was trying to tell us. I won't let anything happen to you."

Right. Her journal. Atticus wanted to protect the journal his father had written in—and, by extension, her, since she seemed to be the only one who could decipher John Kincaid's shorthand. Her stalker was an inconvenience that was getting in the way of them finding the answers they needed.

She should be feeling crushing disappointment that in Atticus's mind, she came in second place to a book. Instead, she was relieved to have a clearer understanding of their relationship. They were friends—partners, even, on this investigation. She didn't have to worry about her plain looks or shy ways or inexperience handling an intimate relationship with a man. As long as she remembered she was a friend and—despite last night's passionate tutoring session—nothing more, then she couldn't set herself up for embarrassment or heartache.

Brave thoughts. Understanding that in the bright light of day she didn't even register on Atticus's babe radar *did* hurt. Combine that whole unrequited attraction to the man with the antsy feeling of knowing she'd snagged the attention of some sicko she *didn't* want, and it made for an isolated, frightened feeling inside her. She reached up to straighten the gold chain that hung at the front of her blouse, and wound up clutching the charm from her father, along with the lock box key she'd strung there beside it. They were symbols of the people she'd cared about whom she'd already lost.

Don't let Brooke go with her mother. Her own father wanted her to live, to fight, to thrive.

Why was she worrying about bruised egos or misguided feelings when she stood to lose so much more?

Brooke circled around the center island to pour herself a mug of coffee while she put things into perspective. "The laughing man knows where I live, doesn't he?" She turned and faced Atticus across the island. "Do you think he'll come here? Are Peggy and Louise, or any of Mr. McCarthy's crew in any danger?"

His steely gaze reached out to her, and for a moment she thought he was going to give her a standard, *It'll be okay.*

But that wasn't Atticus's way. "His contact with you has been escalating. He may still be anonymous, but he's grown bolder, more personal. In his perverted way, he may think he's courting you—that you're enjoying the attention."

"I'm not."

"I know."

"So are Peggy and Lou safe? I didn't tell them about the rest of it. Just the call last night. Do I need to warn them to watch their backs? Or ship them off on one of their trips until this blows over?" She looked down into the bottomless darkness of her coffee. "Am *I* safe? Or is it just a matter of time before he decides to introduce himself in person?"

"Here. Pour me another cup of that." He rose and joined her at the sink. Though he leaned one hip casually against the counter, there was nothing casual about the deep focus of his eyes on her upturned face, nor in the unvarnished clarity of his words. "Every stalker is unique. But Laughing Man seems to be following a pretty textbook pattern."

"Which is?"

"He likes the thrill of this *relationship* he's creating with you. It probably seems real—and mutual—to him. I imagine he's getting off on the control he has over your emotions. He's transferring your fear into attraction, maybe even caring."

Sickened by the notion that that creep was feeding off her fright and paranoia, Brooke tipped her face up to Atticus, trying to find some good news. "So if I stop reacting, he goes away?"

But there wasn't any to find. "If you blow him off, he's probably going to see that as a rejection of his attention. And that might piss him off, make him less predictable. That's when I'd worry about your aunts being used in some kind of retaliation. Or him becoming physically aggressive toward you."

"You really don't know how to give a pep talk, do you? So, in order to protect the people I love, I have to let him terrorize me for the rest of my life?" She set her mug on the counter, freeing her arms to try to hug away the chill that possibility generated.

Atticus's mug went down beside hers before he turned her to face him. He rubbed his hands up and down her arms, instilling a warmth and strength she couldn't find. "I'm not going anywhere until I figure this out and I have a man in handcuffs. I put in a call to Patrol Division to swing by the house every hour. They'll also be looking for anyone loitering in the neighborhood who shouldn't be. I've got Sawyer tracking your phone records for last night's call, and Holden has a couple of days off and promised to help keep an eye on the place. Plus, I've started a database search for previous offenders who fit the profile."

"You did all that this morning?"

"I get things done. I'm not messing around with this guy and your safety." Meaning, he wouldn't let anything happen to the journal, or her ability to crack the code inside for him. "I also think you should tell Major Taylor about the flowers and messages."

Brooke shook her head and tried to pull away. "He'll think I'm some kind of flake. And I'm trying to show him how competent—"

"He'll think you're smart to be taking proactive steps to protect yourself. He'll watch over you like a hawk at the office. The more people we have working on this, the sooner we'll get results." His grip tightened around her shoulders, nearly lifting her onto her toes. His steely gaze commanded hers. "We'll find who this bastard is and get a restraining order. Then, if he so much as breathes in your direction, I will lock him up."

Brooke stroked her fingers down the placket of his shirt. It was almost like petting a rangy jungle cat—all coiled energy with the threat of violence thrumming right beneath the surface. She wanted to understand the edgy tension in his voice—wanted to ease it. "I can't ask you to do all that for me. You have your own job. Your own life. You should concentrate on finding John's killer, not worry about my little problem."

"There is nothing *little* about a man terrorizing an innocent woman." Atticus brushed the backs of his fingers beneath her jaw, taking the sharpness from his words. "We'll find him and expose him. Take away his power."

Spreading her hands against the hard warmth of his chest, Brooke fought the urge to lay her cheek there instead. "What do I do in the meantime? Just pray I don't say or do the wrong thing?"

He traced the curve of her hairline, catching a curly tendril of hair and tucking it gently behind her ear. "I promised my mother I'd look out for you. That's not a word I can go back on. I won't let him hurt you."

Ah, yes. Funny how a man could add insult to injury, yet make her admire him all the more at the same time.

Brooke curled her fingers into her palms and turned away to pull out a bowl and some cereal she didn't feel like eating. "That's awfully nice for Susan to be concerned."

"Brooke. What that means is I won't break my word to you, either. You're too important to my family. And I've—"

A knock at the back door ended the conversation abruptly. Everything inside Brooke froze, but Atticus was already moving.

"Damn." He checked his watch. "McCarthy's men aren't due for another half hour."

Louise shouted from her bedroom. "That'll be for me!" She and Peggy must have been hiding out in order to give Brooke some alone time with Atticus. Averting her eyes as though hoping she was interrupting a romantic moment, Louise breezed through the kitchen. "You two go about your business. I'll get it."

"I've got it." Atticus snatched the journal off the counter and pushed it into Brooke's hands.

"No, really. I—"

But Atticus was already at the door, blocking Louise's grasp and preventing Brooke from seeing their early-morning visitor. "What do you want, Fierro?"

"Well, if it isn't Brooke's friend." Tony Fierro's voice

was about as friendly as Atticus's wary posture. "Good morning to you, too."

"Detective!" Louise protested, uselessly pulling at Atticus's arm. "Let him in."

"Atticus." The instinct to protect her aunt—even from Atticus's refuse-to-budge demeanor—finally pumped some fire into Brooke's veins. "Don't you think you're overreacting?"

"What do you want?" Atticus repeated, each word a well-placed bullet.

"Cool your jets, detective. I haven't broken any law. I'm here for Miss Louise." Brooke could see the dark blue of Tony's bandanna head-wrap over Atticus's shoulder now. His posture must have puffed up to meet Atticus's unwavering stance. "She's expecting me."

"What's going on?" Peggy had joined them as well. The concern in her voice prompted Brooke to take action. "Has something else happened?"

"Something else?" Tony's voice lost its flippant edge and colored with concern. "Is anything wrong, ma'am?"

"It's okay, Aunt Peg," Brooke hastened to reassure her. "It's just a misunderstanding."

Summoning the strength to move—to be *proactive* about taking charge of her life—Brooke reached up and cupped Atticus's shoulder. His muscles bunched beneath her touch, and the urge to pull back skittered across her skin. But she refused to retreat. "Please." She didn't know what kind of influence, if any, she had over him, but if she could diffuse the distrust and dislike that had blossomed between the two men, she would. "He *does* work for us. He has a right to be here. And you're scaring Peggy and Lou."

"Somebody around here should be scared." Atticus angled his jaw toward her but didn't budge. "What do you really know about this guy? I've tried to find out and have come up with next to nothing."

"You checked me out?" Tony taunted.

"Ex-con? Three women? What do you think?"

Peggy walked up between Brooke and Louise, peering around Atticus. "Brooke received a disturbing phone call last night, and Atticus is understandably concerned about who we let into our home."

"Disturbing? Hey, it wasn't me. Is that what you think?" Tony actually retreated a step onto the deck, wanting to put them at ease. Brooke watched his face go unnaturally pale. "I wouldn't make a crank call like that, ma'am. And you know me better than that. Right, Miss Louise?" He held up his hands, turning his argument on Atticus. "I'll give you my cell number. You can check the phone records—I never called here last night."

"Oh, I will."

"Think about it logically, Atticus." Brooke tried reason when her personal appeal failed. "He can't be our man. Even if he called from another phone, I'd have recognized Tony's voice."

Atticus's shoulders rose and fell with a long, controlled breath. "You have a lot to learn about self-preservation, honey."

"And you have a lot to learn about having faith in people."

Atticus's unsmiling countenance took in all three women before turning back to their visitor. "Fine. I'll let you three outvote me this time. But don't expect to stay long."

The last remark was for Tony before Atticus stepped

aside. But he didn't move far, just a few feet back to retrieve his coffee and position himself at the sink so he could keep an eye on everything—and everyone—in the kitchen area.

Finding she was a little leery of Atticus's watchful gaze herself, Brooke left to stick the journal in her purse. When she returned, she poured milk over her cereal and carried the bowl around to the far side of the island to sit. Though it tasted like straw on her tongue, she forced herself to eat. The effort wasn't just about nutrition, but about the need to withdraw to a quiet place inside herself for a few minutes. Atticus must be counting on her more than she'd imagined to help uncover any clue as to John's murder. The pressure to be successful was almost as keen as the disappointment she felt at confirming his protection over her wasn't as personally motivated as she might have hoped.

Atticus cared about her. But he didn't… care. Not the way she wanted him to. Not the way she—*oh, my God*—loved… him. She quickly jabbed a spoonful of milk and straw into her mouth, needing some kind of sensation besides the pain whipping through her. After only a couple of kisses, had she really expected some kind of miracle to happen?

And the world went on around her despite the heartache she was feeling.

"I picked up that tiller you ordered, Miss Louise." Tony Fierro handed Louise a rental receipt. "I know we just have it for the day, so I wanted to get an early start. Besides, if the temperature is steaming up to a hundred degrees again today, I want to get the hardest of that sod-breaking done this morning while it's still relatively cool."

"Sounds like a plan, Tony." Louise linked her arm around the twisting serpents that seemed to crawl with each ripple of Tony's hard muscles, and escorted him to a metal stool. "But not until you eat some breakfast. Did you have donuts again?"

"No, ma'am. Just a cup of coffee."

"I thought so. Can't expect a day's work of a man who hasn't had a decent breakfast. Now sit." She tilted her chin toward Atticus, her expression indicating that she found his hosting skills suspect. "Is that all right with you, Detective?"

His gaze never left Tony. "Breakfast is fine."

"Peggy? How about another plate?"

Tony hesitated until Louise pushed his shoulder and urged him onto a stool at the opposite end of the counter from Brooke. He didn't need to be asked twice as his pale face warmed with a smile. "Is that bacon I smell?"

Peggy retied her apron and set about melting some butter in the fry pan. "It sure is. One working man's special coming up."

"So, Fierro," the cop in Atticus wouldn't rest, "where were you last night between, say, midnight and 1:00 a.m.?"

Please. Maybe he should just tell a joke to see if Tony's laugh sounded familiar. But Atticus seemed incapable of even smiling this morning. Brooke caught her necklace up in her fist and worked the chain between her fingers, seeking an outlet to dispel the awkward discomfort building inside her.

"I was at home in my apartment," Tony answered. "I put in a full day of hard labor out in the heat yesterday. I was passed out by eleven. And no, no one can vouch for me. But like I said, the phone records will show that I didn't make any calls to anybody last night."

"How many pancakes will you eat?" Peggy interrupted, no doubt feeling the same tension that was driving Brooke into her shell, judging by the vigor with which she was stirring that batter.

"However many you want to serve, ma'am. A home-cooked meal is a real treat for me."

"Make him a stack of four, Peg," Louise ordered, setting out a glass and pouring milk.

With her aunts bustling about the kitchen, the ensuing lull in the conversation didn't register until Tony spoke again. "Where'd you get that?"

Brooke stopped chewing when she realized the handyman was looking at her. No, *staring* at the charm that dangled between her fingers.

A ripple of unease cascaded down her spine at the unwelcome scrutiny. Swallowing the last lump of food she could manage, she curled the necklace into her palm and tucked it back inside her blouse. "The charm is a family heirloom. My father gave it to me when I was born."

"Who's your father?" Odd. Freaky odd that a relative stranger would be so interested in something of hers.

"Leo Hansford. He passed away when I was a baby." Her gaze slid over to Atticus, who stood up straight and was watching the exchange with an intense interest. "The charm belonged to my mother."

"Your mother?" Tony's gaze never wavered from her chest.

Brooke's spoon clattered in her bowl. "Do you mind not staring at me like that, please?"

"Sorry, ma'am." Tony turned his attention to the plate Peggy set in front of him. Louise had brought him his milk, too, before he spoke again. "I lost my mother when I was ten. I never got anything to remember her by."

"I'm sorry to hear that." Perhaps growing up without a strong parental influence had led to his spree of robberies and eventually prison.

"In my head, I'll never forget what she looked like, though." His gaze wandered back to Brooke and lingered. She'd been watched like this before. From a distance.

She hadn't even known Tony then. But she knew him now. He was studying her face. Watching. "Mr. Fierro!"

He picked up his fork and attacked the pancakes and bacon Peggy set in front of him. "My bad. I sometimes forget my manners when I get around a pretty lady."

Pretty lady. "What did you say?"

That drained the blood right out of her.

"Brooke." But before words could form, before a coherent thought could get past the instant panic that phrase stirred in her head, Atticus was there. He pulled out the stool between her and Tony and sat. "Dish me up another plate of those pancakes, too, Peg."

"Aren't you worried about being late for work?" Peggy asked. "I thought you needed to be on the highway by seven-thirty."

"Nope." He was completely in charge, completely cool, completely in control of the entire room. He slid his hand beneath the edge of the counter and wrapped his comforting grip around her ice-cold fingers. "I'm not not going anywhere until McCarthy and his men get here."

I'm not leaving any of you alone with this man.

Brooke tried to get back to that rational place of self-reliance inside her head. It couldn't have been Tony's voice on the telephone. And while the bulky build of the man she'd seen in the truck that first day made her think of Tony, she couldn't remember seeing any tattoos. And that man in the purple K-State cap had been blond. Tony's dark hair and dark eyes spoke of his Mediterranean heritage.

As someone who'd often wished the same for herself, Brooke had been adamant about giving Tony the benefit of the doubt. Yes, he had a criminal record. But he'd served his time, and he'd been employed without complaint by Truman McCarthy for nearly a year. He was sweet to her aunts, respectful to her, and had done the work of two men since signing on as their handyman.

But had she been too trusting, too naive, to insist on hiring him? For three days she hadn't thought so. He was rough around the edges, yes, but she'd always thought he looked more solitary than sinister.

He looked a hell of a lot scarier, though, when she imagined that *he* could be the man on the other end of that phone call last night.

She altered her grip and hung on tight to Atticus's hand.

Chapter Ten

"You know I can't give you that information, Detective Kincaid."

Atticus hadn't really expected much help from FBI Agent Riley Holt, but he figured it was worth a shot to call in the favor. Atticus and his brothers—Sawyer, in particular—had helped Agent Holt in his manhunt for three escaped prisoners earlier that year. Learning that one of the fugitives was Ace Longbow, the ex-husband of Sawyer's wife, Melissa, had made joining Holt and his team a personal mission. Though Longbow had ended up dead in a hostage standoff, Holt had ended up smelling like a rose, maintaining his image as the Bureau's resident golden boy.

He owed the Kincaids a favor.

"But you know something about Fierro, don't you?" Atticus had reasoned out that a man could erase his past in one of two ways—either he was a relocated government witness in a protection program, in which case, Holt could access the information—or he was a bad guy with some very powerful, very covert connections. The kind of connections that nobody—not a veteran cop like his father, and certainly not an innocent woman like Brooke—should be messing with.

He was praying for the witness angle.

"There's some sketchy information on his background I can share." Holt's voice dropped to a hush as Atticus passed a slow-moving truck on the interstate. His drive to K.C.'s latest crime scene at the landfill south of town had offered him the private time to make the call to Holt's office in Chicago. He held his breath and waited. "Fierro is in the watch files with several aliases. He always uses Antonio as his first name, but Fierro is only one of a dozen surnames we've searched under. He was born in Europe, but I can't even tell you if he's Italian."

"You can't tell me or you don't know?" Another mile marker sped by as Holt paused. Atticus checked his rearview mirror and pulled back into the driving lane. His turnoff was coming up fast, and then he'd have to focus on the body a bulldozer operator had found. His time was running out. "Holt. I'm a bright enough boy to figure out Fierro isn't who he says he is. Can you tell me if he has a record of crimes against women? Stalking? Assault? Rape?"

"Here's what I *can* tell you. Fierro's not in the witness relocation program."

Atticus swore. One word. Pithy and to the point. "Thanks, Holt. Let me know if you find anything on Fierro."

"Yeah." After disconnecting the call, Atticus hooked his phone back on his belt. So Fierro was a very, very bad guy. A watch list meant he could even be connected to a terrorist cell.

What the hell was he supposed to do with information

like that? Show Brooke the forged birth certificate? And say what? I can't prove who your hired man is, but since I don't like him, fire his ass. Hell. That would make a lousy argument. Atticus believed in his gut that Tony Fierro meant trouble for Brooke and her aunts. But he was a cop. A man of reason. He needed facts to prove his case.

And while he was solving life's mysteries, what the hell was he supposed to do with Brooke herself?

Besides keeping her safe. Beyond tapping into that clever brain of hers. Atticus wasn't a man who was easily stumped by a puzzle. But Brooke Hansford had his thoughts spinning in circles.

She wasn't plain so much as he'd never taken the time to notice that she wasn't. The warm caramel color of her hair, which, when the curls were freed from their practical bun, seemed to have a delightful mind of their own.

Not unlike the woman herself.

He'd known Brooke for years, but was just now discovering the real beauty of her big green eyes, the way she was always thinking—sometimes overthinking—but always engaged in the people and things around her. The soft, true-green irises spoke of an intelligence that aroused him, that awoke an enticing challenge in him to explore those thoughts and match those mental dynamics by stepping up his own intellectual game.

He'd spent too many years thinking of Brooke as a pleasant enough addition to his circle of family and friends. But over these past few days, she'd created unexpected tidal waves in his ordered, predictable world. She laughed off her clumsiness, picked herself up and kept moving forward. She guarded a secret well of passion and threw herself into a kiss with an abandon that was unpolished natural talent and utterly hot.

And that body. He blew out a slow, steadying breath at the way things kicked to attention south of his belt buckle just thinking of her long, lithe limbs wrapped around him. Last night, she'd cradled his hips against her most feminine warmth as her pert little breasts beaded to attention and branded his chest with the evidence of her desire. If he hadn't come to his senses—remembered the time, the aunts' impending arrival, and just how hard a granite countertop could be—they would have christened that kitchen.

And lived to regret it in the morning.

She'd been totally turned on last night, maybe more than even she realized. Her guileless enthusiasm had been a total turn-on for him, as well. Forget about the psych it was to his male ego to have no doubts about how much a woman wanted him, it had been surprisingly refreshing—almost cleansing to his soul somehow—to realize that Brooke Hansford wasn't playing any games with him. She probably didn't even know how to play the games that Hayley had used to make a fool of him.

He'd been surprised when she'd first initiated that kiss, then curious to see how much she knew, how far she'd go. He'd invited her to repeat the experiment, thinking he'd teach her a thing or two about kissing. But somehow, he ended up as the very willing student.

What Brooke lacked in style, she made up for in raw, unfiltered passion. There was something about her innocence, her enthusiasm, that had slipped beneath his jaded hide. He'd been so on guard against another Hayley poisoning his life that he never saw Brooke coming.

Now she was here. In his thoughts, under his skin, perilously close to something much more vulnerable and irrational—even deeper inside him. She was an undiscovered treasure who could be his for the taking.

Which was the heart of the problem. The cause for a restless night's sleep and a cold shower this morning.

He might be the vigilant explorer who had discovered the secret passions and hidden beauty of Brooke Hansford. But with that discovery came an unexpected responsibility. Family friend. Like a daughter to his late father. He'd promised his mother he'd take care of her, for damn sake.

How did he go about creating a relationship when everyone was counting on him to maintain the status quo? What if said relationship didn't work out? Did he risk upsetting the family vibe when they were just beginning to come out of the dark hole that had captured them all after his father's death? He'd be a marked man if he wound up hurting Brooke. And after all she'd done for the Kincaids, that'd be one hell of a heap of guilt he'd have to live with if he said or did anything to cause her pain.

And what about Brooke herself? If she was the kind of woman who'd settle for a weekend fling, then he'd turn in his badge. He had her pegged as one of those old-fashioned, forever kind of women. After Hayley, he was probably too damn cynical to really believe in forever. But Brooke deserved nothing less.

He'd be smarter with his emotions the next time he tried a relationship. Maybe he could turn off that part of him and just enjoy the physical aspect of what Brooke had offered. They could have some fun as he taught her about sex and intimacy. She'd spruced up her hair and glasses, had tapped into an inner strength and growing confidence. It seemed a logical next step—school her in the arts of desire, then walk away with no regrets. Let some other man be the lucky recipient of Brooke's beautiful smiles and untapped passion.

"Hell." Atticus swerved, nearly driving past his exit as he envisioned the possibility of Brooke wrapping herself around another man the way she'd embraced him last night. That idea sat about as well as knowing his father's killer was still a free man.

BROOKE DREADED opening the mail this morning. But with Mitch Taylor standing right beside her, and her buddy, Mirza Patel, tinkering with her computer at her desk, she had plenty of support around her to accomplish the task.

She finally inhaled a deep breath after the last envelope revealed nothing more disturbing than yet another report Mitch had been asked to write. "You know, it's been something different each time—the roses, the note, the call, following me—maybe I don't have to worry about any more bizarre messages."

Mitch took the stack of letters from her hands. "And maybe it means he's ready to step it up to something more dangerous."

"What is it with you cops and your pep talks?" She tried to raise a smile, but her facial muscles railed against the effort.

"It can be unpredictable work. But understanding what you may be up against improves your chances of survival and success."

"You're right, of course." While she appreciated Mitch's kindly yet straightforward approach to their working relationship, she missed the centering calm she felt when Atticus touched her arm or squeezed her hand or brushed her hair off her face. They were subtle touches, yet very personal, very intimate connections that hinted at the strength and depth of the man behind the touch. She could use a little of that strength to ground the edgy, unsettled feeling plaguing her this morning.

"All the same, we'll make this part of our daily routine for now," Mitch continued. "And if you receive anything like that at home, put it in a plastic bag to preserve any prints or DNA evidence, and call Atticus or bring it in to me."

"You don't think there's any chance that he'll lose interest and stop harassing me?" Atticus hadn't thought so, and she could read the agreement on Mitch's stern face even before he answered.

"It's been my experience that a stalker won't stop until you stop him." And how was she supposed to do that? Mitch sorted through the papers one more time, handing off one memo for Brooke to answer and carrying the others to his in-box. She followed him into his office, jotting down further instructions for the remainder of the day. A few minutes later, Mitch pulled his jacket from the coatrack beside the door and shrugged it on over his shoulders. "If you leave the building for any reason—even just to go down the street for lunch—I want you to tell me, or the desk sergeant if I'm not here. I want to be able to track you down in an instant, no matter where you are."

Brooke smiled. Though he didn't offer the comfort she craved from a certain detective, her new boss was every bit the watchdog Atticus had claimed he would be. "Yes, sir."

"What did I say about that sir stuff?" Mitch offered her

an indulgent smile. "Don't think you're doing me any favors by keeping quiet about this. Atticus was right to have you tell me about these contacts. If someone in my office is being harassed, then I'm being harassed. And I don't take too kindly to that."

"Thanks, Mitch. It's nice to know I won't have to worry about that…issue… here are work."

He nodded toward Mirza. "Now you go back to your computer training. I'm heading out to my lunch meeting with the commissioner. If you leave, remember, tell Sergeant Wheeler."

"I will." Though still somewhat rattled by this morning's strange encounter with Tony Fierro, Brooke felt a little more settled in her own skin knowing that she not only had the Kincaid family in her corner, but she now had a precinct chief looking out for her. If Tony was up to something, as Atticus suspected—if anyone was up to something—she'd have plenty of people watching her back. With no new messages in the mail or phone calls to haunt her, maybe she could actually get some work done yet this morning. She turned to her former classmate. "So, you promised to show me a shortcut in the presentation program."

Mirza's white teeth gleamed against his tanned skin as he smiled. "Yes. Of course, you can follow the documentation in the manual, but I have shortcuts for every aspect of this system that I know you will enjoy."

An hour or so later, Brooke had already pieced together a mock presentation and customized the layout of her desktop when she hit the first glitch in the Caldwell Tech software. She frowned at the frozen screen. "It's locking up when I type in my password to access my e-mail. Is there a default I need to access before I can personalize all my settings?"

"No, it shouldn't…" Mirza's black eyebrows came together like two woolly caterpillars. "Let me try something." He typed in a series of command codes, but the screen didn't so much as blink. Brooke asked if simply rebooting the program would clear the system. He shook his head, still frowning. "You'd lose all of the settings you just created."

"Not a problem. I could easily recreate them—I had a good teacher who showed me how."

Mirza ignored the compliment and climbed under the desk to follow a bundle of cords to the wall behind her. "Did I forget to connect the access wire?"

Brooke rolled her chair out of the way and asked, "Did you find the cord you left in here yesterday? Detective Kincaid said you came back to my office after I'd left to pick up some equipment you'd left behind."

"No. I found it in my case, after all. I had put it in the wrong compartment." Mirza pulled a pair of snips from his belt and continued to work. "Your detective friend gave me quite a fright. I thought he was going to arrest me."

"Atticus can be very protective. More intimidating than he realizes, I think. But he's just being a—" she wouldn't fool herself "—a good friend."

Mirza's soft cheer diverted her attention from going down the frustrations of Heartache Row again. "Try it now."

Brooke entered her password, and nearly fainted at the first message scrolling onto her screen.

MY PRETTY LADY in block letters across the top of the e-mail was the least of her worries.

The soft laughter clogged her ears and grew to a deafening roar inside her head.

There was her face—a recent photo, taken from a distance—with the limestone walls of her home in the background.

And then… Brooke clutched her hand over her mouth as her stomach twisted into a sickened knot. The rational part of her brain knew that half-naked body wasn't hers. She knew the lily-white arms holding that body had never held hers. She knew the cuts, the mutilation, the blood—weren't her.

But it was her face spliced into the graphic image on her computer screen.

It was *her* terror welling up in her throat.

"What's this? A reminder so you don't lock yourself out at night?"

Brooke felt the hand at her neck and screamed.

She jumped back from the unwelcome touch, knocked her chair over, wiped out the blotter and jar of pens and pencils from the top of her desk.

"Whoa. Whoa. Whoa." Mirza was pale beneath his tan. He held up his hands in surrender as he stood. "I'm sorry. I'm sorry. I did not mean to touch you."

She'd screamed. This room would be swarming with cops in two seconds. They'd see that awful picture. Mirza could turn around and see that awful picture.

Acting on pure instinct, Brooke reached around her friend and hit a key to hide the picture on the screen. Maggie Wheeler, the desk sergeant, was suddenly at the door. Brooke waved that she was okay. "I'm sorry. I just got startled. And then I knocked stuff over. But I'm okay. False alarm."

"You're sure?" Maggie looked as tough as any male counterpart with her blue uniform and six-foot stature. She didn't seem to know whether to keep her eye on Brooke or Mirza.

Brooke glanced over and saw that Mirza's hands were still raised in surrender. No wonder Maggie was suspicious. "Put your hands down." When Mirza slowly lowered his hands to his sides, Brooke turned to Maggie again. She'd already sensed the possibility of making a friend here, but not if she continued to come across as paranoid or flighty. "I'm sorry, Maggie. There was a crude picture on the screen, and I overreacted."

Maggie tucked her ash-blond hair into her ponytail. "Stuff like that isn't supposed to get through the KCPD filters."

Brooke pointed up at Mirza. "Well, I've got the tech guy here. I'll have him look into it. I promise, I'm fine."

After all, a picture couldn't hurt her, could it?

"Detective Kincaid is out at a crime scene, but if you want I can call him."

And tell him what? Laughing Man had raised the stakes again? What could Atticus do but look at the sick photo, too? She'd save it in a file as evidence, but she wouldn't call him away from his job just to hold her hand. Forcing herself to breathe evenly again, willing her pulse to steady, she adjusted her glasses on her nose and smiled. "I'll contact Detective Kincaid myself. Thanks, Maggie."

With a nod, Maggie reluctantly returned to her post at the sergeant's desk and Brooke stooped down to pick up the mess she'd made. "I'm sorry, Mirza. You asked me a question?"

He crawled beside her to help with the cleanup. "The key around your neck. Do you wear it so you do not lose it?"

The key.

Brooke clutched it and sat back on her haunches. She mentally replayed the events at the house that morning. It wasn't the charm Tony Fierro had been ogling, and it certainly wasn't the cleavage. "It's the key."

"Yes, the key." Mirza misinterpreted her thoughts. "I was asking about it."

Brooke pushed to her feet and reached for the telephone. Tony Fierro had served time for robbery. Did he think the key was an opportunity to steal from them? Did he think they'd hidden a strongbox at the house? That this tiny key could give him access to three women's fortunes?

Or was it possible that Tony Fierro knew exactly what that key was for, and who had planted it in her home?

She apparently had a long way to go to be as smart about people as Atticus was.

The phone at the house rang until the answering machine picked up. That was reassuring. Not. Peggy and Louise could be working outside or running errands. But she'd feel a lot safer about them being at the house with Tony if she could warn them of her suspicions. She left a message for them to call her ASAP and then hung up.

"I am so buying them cell phones for their birthdays this year," she muttered, crossing to dig her own phone from the depths of her purse. She didn't want to worry. Louise had probably gone off on some design tangent and Peggy was busy arguing a more sensible, affordable alternative. They were preoccupied with their own business, that was all.

She hoped that was all.

"Brooke, is something wrong?" Mirza had righted her chair and was shutting down her e-mail. "Is there something I can do to help?"

Hold that thought, she indicated, holding up one finger. Once she found Truman McCarthy's number on her cell phone, she dialed it. After three rings, the contractor picked up. "Mr. McCarthy? Brooke Hansford here. Are my aunts around the house, by any chance? I just tried to call."

His impatient huff sounded as though she'd interrupted something important, but his deep voice was as polite and professional as always. "I sent them out to run some errands."

"You did?"

She didn't expect the apology that followed. "I don't know what the trouble is yet, but we ran into some wiring problems this morning. Either something disconnected or we hit a juncture when we were installing the floor vents. I've got an electrician down in the crawl space now. We'll get it taken care of and get it cleaned up so you can sleep here tonight."

Floor vents? She thought Louise's streamlined design called for all the vents to be in the arched ceiling. "Why would someone cut a hole in the floor?"

Mr. McCarthy's laugh was a wry one. "Well, I saw your handiwork over the sunporch door this morning. I was beginning to think your aunt Louise had found something else she didn't like about my work."

"Sorry about that. Something got sealed in when you were putting up the new archway."

"Oh? Did you find it?"

"Yes. But I didn't realize there was a problem with the electricity. Everything worked fine this morning."

"It was a surprise to me, too. I thought we were going to get started on laying the flooring upstairs, but this will take most of the day to make sure all the wiring is ship-shape from top to bottom before we close it in."

"I understand. I'm glad you're there to take care of it."

Maybe she shouldn't be sharing so much information with McCarthy, but until she could reach her aunts, she had to trust someone. "Mr. McCarthy…is Tony Fierro still there working?"

What would she say when McCarthy put him on the line?

"He left with your aunts about an hour ago. Took his truck and they drove your car. They're at the nursery picking out flowers to plant in the garden."

Brooke didn't remember thanking him or saying goodbye. But the dread pumping through her veins charged her heart with adrenaline and cleared her head to what she must do next.

She walked straight out to Atticus's desk and verified what Maggie had told her, that he was out on a call. She started to jot a quick note—*Find me*. But Atticus and Major Taylor both had made it clear that she should contact one of them if she heard from Laughing Man again. So Brooke flipped open her cell and dialed Atticus's number.

Voice mail. Damn. She had a hard enough time carrying on a conversation sometimes, but there was always something in her brain that froze up the instant a machine beeped and demanded a concise, coherent message. "It's me, Atticus. Brooke. Um…I got an e-mail you'll want to see. I'll meet you at the bank. If you can still make it. At one, maybe? And, um, I'm going to see my aunts. I'm worried about them. Okay? Call me. Or, I'll see you later. Bye."

She rolled her eyes as she ended the message. "That'll make him think I'm an idiot."

She'd been aware of Mirza following her out of the office, so when he touched her arm this time, she didn't jump. "Is everything all right? You are running around like a crazy person."

Crazy maybe. But smart.

She wasn't going to go running off to face Tony Fierro by herself. But she wasn't going to wait to find out if her aunts were safe alone with him, either. She spotted the blond detective sitting at a corner desk and crossed the room to introduce herself.

"Detective Grove? Hi, I'm Brooke Hansford, Major Taylor's new assistant." He stood. And stood. And continued to stand, forcing her to tilt her head back. But his big hand seemed friendly enough as he extended it in greeting.

"Nice to officially meet you, ma'am."

She refused the seat he offered. This wouldn't take long. "You may or may not know that I was John Kincaid's assistant at the time of his…murder."

"I recognize the name."

Brooke nodded. Atticus might shoot her later, but she wasn't going to wait to prove suspicions. "I think John tried to tell me something before he died. Unfortunately, he made a puzzle out of it, so it's taking me some time to find all the pieces and make sense of them."

"You mean something about his murder?" She detected a surprising astuteness behind his prize-fighter's face.

"Possibly. It could wind up being something personal, but if it does have something to do with the investigation into his death, you'd be the man I'd talk to, right?"

"What kind of message are you talking about?"

Brooke held up the safe-deposit-box key. "Atticus and I are going to the Cattlemen's Bank over on Grand Avenue this afternoon to find out. Don't get him into trouble, please. He's only trying to help me. Would you like to join us? It could be nothing, but—"

"It could be everything." Grove nodded. "I'll be there."

"And if I'm late, you'll tell Atticus, right?" You'll call out the troops? Comb the city?

"Yes, ma'am."

"Thanks." Without wasting another breath, Brooke turned around and headed back to her office. She linked her arm through Mirza's and pulled him along with her. "Do you have your car with you?"

"Yes."

"Will you give me a ride?"

"Of course. But tell me what is going on."

"I need to find my aunts right away. I'm worried that something is terribly wrong."

"YOU'VE GOT SOMEBODY else after Brooke Hansford, don't you?"

Antonio's employer rose behind the desk. "What the hell are you doing here? Have you gone mad?"

Their meetings had always been arranged by a phone call, the locations always of the boss's choosing. But this morning, in Brooke Hansford's kitchen, Antonio had heard enough to become suspicious.

He'd seen enough to know the truth. This was more than the routine search-and-retrieval mission he'd been hired to carry out.

This was personal.

"You haven't got Mr. Smith with you to protect you here." Antonio pounded his fist on the desk, rattling the phone and computer, sending papers flying. "So answer the damn question!"

But his boss had been a survivor for far too long to let anger get the better of common sense. Momentary fury at the intrusion quickly faded from the icy eyes.

"Yes."

"You admit it?" His boss gestured to the chair across the desk, but Antonio wasn't here to sit and make nice. Finding out he was right about having competition on this mission didn't ease the sting to his pride. Or his concern about his competitor's tactics. "You're setting me up to be the scape-goat. There's been more than one crank phone call, right? You're terrorizing that woman to throw suspicion onto me so that someone else can fly under the radar and complete the assignment."

Unmoved by his temper, the boss sat. "The profile does fit your history, doesn't it?"

"You erased that from my record."

The boss actually smiled, as if they were sharing an old joke between friends. "Are you telling me you haven't thought about Brooke Hansford in that way? I can make the paperwork go away, but the urge to take, to control, to own a woman in that way has always been your downfall."

Antonio ran his tongue around his lips. It wasn't the virgin herself that had him so frustrated that he was tempted to do violence at the moment. "I have been loyal to you since I was a boy. No one in your organization—no one—has served you better than me. And now you're setting me up to take the fall so that someone else can get the job done?"

"The method is of his own choosing. I have to admire

it, though. There's nothing like a classic misdirection to divert Miss Hansford and the police's attention from the job I need to have done."

"I could have completed the job on my own. I still can."

Manicured fingers drummed impatiently on the desktop. "The information John Kincaid may have written down could destroy everything it has taken me thirty years to build. There are too many secrets, too much money, at stake. Your pride is of no consideration to me. I'm covering my bets."

"It wasn't enough for you to pull the trigger and kill Kincaid?" Antonio finally lowered himself onto the chair, but he perched on the forward edge. "I would have done that for you, too."

"This is business. That was personal. It was my right." Antonio detected the slightest quavering in the boss's tone. The clenched fist tapping the arm of the chair confirmed the rare revelation of honest emotion. "Kincaid betrayed me. He convinced the others that Irina Zorinsky Hansford had to die."

Antonio laughed before he could consider the wisdom of silence. "Do you know that Brooke wears a charm around her neck that belonged to Irina Hansford?" Antonio pulled the ring of keys from his pocket and licked the attached gold charm with his thumb. A charm marked with a Cyrillic Z. "Just like the one my mother gave me." Antonio paused. "Is Brooke Hansford my sister? Is that what John Kincaid found out?"

Raw, blinding emotion passed over his boss's expression. "Irina Zorinsky is dead. Her bloodline died with her. Nothing but getting me that information is any concern of yours."

The emotion passed as quickly as it had shown itself.

The boss got up, buttoning the flawlessly cut jacket and walking to the door to open it. Antonio was being dismissed. "I will see the job done. Whether you get me the information or my other operative does, doesn't matter."

It mattered. Antonio was the number-one man here. He'd earned the right to be trusted without question.

But the loyalty that was of such vital importance to him meant nothing to his employer. "I will have whatever Kincaid left for Brooke, and I will bury it forever. The man who brings me that information will be rewarded—handsomely, as usual. The man who fails? Dies."

THE LANDFILL stunk like death.

The bright summer sun cooked everything the bulldozer had overturned until it stunk even worse.

Still, Atticus pulled off his mask as M.E. Holly Masterson approached. "You got anything for me, Doc?"

Holly pulled off her mask as well and stuffed it into her back jeans pocket. "Not much, I'm afraid. The heat has accelerated decomp, and she's been here ten days, maybe two weeks. I'd say she's late fifties, early sixties. I can try to inflate the skin and pull some prints, but don't hold your breath. If she's not in AFIS, then that won't do us any good. And it looks as though she was pretty beat up before she was dumped here. I have a man in the lab who does reconstructive work. We'll see if we can get enough of her teeth together to identify her through dental records."

"Is that the cause of death?" He pulled his notebook from his jacket. "You think it's a domestic situation that got out of control?"

"I can't guess on the abuse aspect yet. I'll know more

when the autopsy's done, but I'm ninety-nine percent sure these are the cause of death." She pulled a small plastic bag from another pocket and showed it to Atticus.

He didn't need his reading glasses to recognize a pair of bullets. "You pulled these slugs out of the body already?"

"It wasn't hard. The wound tracks in her chest and head were so degraded, one of them actually fell out when I turned the body." He handed her the evidence bag and she held them up toward the sunlight. "It's almost like there's some kind of chemical reaction going on. The bullets are disintegrating, eroding the surrounding tissue with them. I doubt ballistics will be able to get any striations off them. The caliber will be hard enough to pin down."

Atticus frowned. "Disintegrating bullets? Are you kidding me?" Bullets exploded, changed shape, fanned out or blunted depending on the size, velocity of the shot and whatever they passed through or hit. Bullets didn't decompose. "You mean they're too damaged to get a read on them?"

"I mean they're melting. Making them damn near impossible to trace." She tucked the bag safely into her pocket.

"Who the hell has technology like that? Sounds like the CIA or MI6 or, hell, is it a mob hit?" Sometimes, they imported some freaky stuff. This made no sense. The heat and stench and confusion were giving him a damn headache.

"You're the detective. I'm the scientist. I'll report what I find, but it's up to you to turn the information into answers."

"Thanks." Leaving the crime scene to Holly and her lab crew, Atticus crunched his way across the layers of trash and filth and new dirt, heading for his SUV parked on the gravel road that circled the fill.

"Detective Kincaid?" Holly had run up behind him. She

tucked her short, dark hair behind one ear and took a deep breath. He wasn't going to like whatever she had to say. "I've seen bullets like these before."

"This murder is connected to another crime scene?"

"Possibly." Her hazel eyes gleamed with a certain intelligence and hesitation similar to a pair of beautiful green eyes that seemed awfully far away right now.

"Spit it out."

Holly nodded. "I pulled two untraceable bullets like these from your father's body. And from a black man named James McBride."

Everything inside Atticus went on full alert. "The same two bodies you found that number three tattoo on."

"How do you know…?" She shook her head. The Kincaids weren't supposed to have details like that. "Never mind. I know those aren't your cases, but—"

"Thanks, Doc. Include the information in your report and send it to me ASAP. And you'd better send a copy to Kevin Grove."

With a nod, Holly turned and picked her way back down the slope while Atticus climbed inside his SUV.

He loosened his tie and collar and cranked the A/C. But he was still feeling little relief from the heat. "Damn."

Nothing about his father's murder made any sense. A string of deaths. No concrete motive. Bullets that couldn't be traced. Cryptic clues in a secretary's journal.

He had nothing but questions. Speculation. Possibilities.

He needed something in his world to start making sense. He needed closure. Order. He needed…to talk to Brooke to get his head back in the right place.

Just thinking about hearing her voice eased the tightness

in his chest. He pulled his phone off his belt to look up her number, relieved he had that connection to her now. He could already feel her gentleness calming him, her klutziness amusing him, her intelligence amazing him.

He could imagine what another kiss would cost his conscience, but it was a risk he was willing to take. Yes. He wanted to kiss Brooke again. He wanted to take his time about doing it, too. He wanted to be very, very thorough, and then they'd try another kiss her way. They'd try several. And he'd get those legs involved somehow, too.

There was a little chink in the feel-good moment when he saw the voice message from her. There was a big damn chink when he listened to the message. He shifted the SUV into Drive and hit the gas, spinning rocks out behind him until the tires found traction and he shot down the road toward the highway.

"I told her to stay put. I told her I'd pick her up. I told her we'd go to the bank together."

Talk about not making sense!

What a hell of a time for the shy Miss Hansford to start asserting that inner strength. She'd gotten an e-mail? Had to be from Laughing Man, judging by the little quiver he imagined in her voice. And she was *worried* about her aunts? Hell. Tony Fierro was with Peggy and Louise all day long. What kind of mess could they have gotten into between breakfast and lunch?

He could easily imagine the worst.

Atticus considered sticking the siren on top of his car, but then that would mean he was truly worried Brooke was getting herself into some kind of trouble, and he wasn't prepared to go there. He wasn't ready to think that

Brooke could be in danger, that she could be hurt. That Laughing Man…

"Don't go there."

Tracks of black rubber followed him onto the highway as Atticus stuck the magnetic light on top of his car and hit the siren on the dashboard.

Chapter Eleven

"Just come quietly with me and get in the car." Brooke took the bulky blue enamel pot Louise refused to put down and urged her aunts to hurry away from the counter where she'd found them paying their bill.

Thankfully, Wolferman's Nursery was a sprawling complex with rows of trees, piles of landscaping rock and clay pots of every size and color to mask their quick-paced walk to the parking lot. Brooke was counting on the displays of annuals and perennials and plenty of customers to hide the fact that three women were trying to sneak away from an ex-con stalker.

As soon as she'd seen Tony Fierro wheel a cart crammed with plants and supplies out to his truck in the loading area, Brooke had dashed up to the counter. Shushing their surprise and waiting impatiently while they collected their receipt, Brooke warned them to be quiet and ushered them out of the greenhouse building in the opposite direction.

She'd asked Mirza to drive around the parking lot until she spotted her own blue VW. Then she'd asked him to park in the nearest spot, several yards away, and wait until she returned with her aunts and was safely inside her car.

Brooke offered him a subtle wave of thanks when she spotted him still standing beside his car.

"Who's your friend?" Louise asked, missing nothing.

Hopping off the curb, Brooke decided to use the key itself to unlock the doors instead of allowing the telltale beep of the remote on her key chain to alert Tony to the fact they were leaving. She shifted the five-gallon pot onto one hip and stuck the key in the lock and turned it. "A classmate of mine from my assertiveness training. He was working with me at the office today and agreed to give me a ride here. He said he'd wait to make sure we got into my car before he left. Get in."

Louise pushed the seat forward and climbed onto the narrow back seat. She reached for the pot Brooke handed to her, twisted it one direction, then the other, then pushed it back. "Turn it around and give me the top end first to see if we can get it in."

Grunting her frustration, Brooke took the weight of the pot and turned it around. Louise looked out the back window, eyeing Mirza again. "He's very exotic-looking, isn't he? Dark and swarthy. If you like that type. There was a time in college when I was in Turkey—"

"Please, Louise. Tell me your exploits later." Brooke handed off the pot and turned a 360, surveying the parking lot over the roofs of the cars. No sign of Tony and his tattoos. His green truck was still in the circular loading drive, but the cart was gone. He'd be taking it back to the counter, looking for her aunts now. Brooke's heartbeat quickened with the countdown toward being discovered.

Louise was taking far too long to settle in with her purchase. She took over wrestling the pot into the back seat. "Slide across and unlock Aunt Peggy's door. I really want to be out of here before Tony realizes you've snuck off."

Peg waited patiently at the opposite side of the car, carefully folding her long receipt and sliding it into her billfold. "I like Detective Kincaid better. What kind of friend doesn't even come over to introduce himself to us? Your detective has better manners."

Louise pushed open the door and debated the point. "She did say she met him in her assertiveness training class. Maybe this Mirza is shy like Brooke. I imagine the two of us can be pretty intimidating if you're not used to confident women."

"We are not—"

"Please, ladies!" Brooke chided them with as much force as her hushed voice would allow. "Tony Fierro wants something from me. And I'm ninety-nine percent sure that he's the one calling and sending me those horrible messages."

"Horrible?" Peggy frowned with concern. "What messages are you talking about?"

"Has Tony threatened you?"

"Please!"

"Miss Louise? Miss Peggy?" Tony was coming.

Every cell inside Brooke seized up. She heard him speaking to the clerk at the counter, probably asking where her aunts had gone. *Think, Brooke. Act. You have to get to Atticus. He's waiting for you at the bank.* And then the adrenaline kicked in and Brooke forgot that she had ever been shy. "Get in the car now. Lock the doors. Hurry."

"Miss Louise?" Tony's voice was louder. He was

coming this way. "Where'd you go? I've got the last of the potted trees loaded in my truck. Miss Peggy…?"

Brooke was vaguely aware of Mirza climbing into his car and driving away. She was completely aware of the man with the designer skin stepping onto the sidewalk. Tony's gaze followed the path of the departing car. Took note of her aunts inside the VW. Locked onto hers.

"Where are you going, Miss Brooke?"

Screw the pot. Brooke set it on the pavement beside her, shoved her seat back into place and tossed her purse inside.

But a cruel vise of fingers cinched around her upper arm and pulled her out before she could get the door shut. Tony slammed the door and slammed her back even harder against it, pinning her with his hips and thighs while his free hand went to her throat. "Where are you going, bitch!"

"Brooke!"

"Tony! Stop that!"

"Get in her purse, Peggy. Find her cell phone."

"I'm just picking up my aunts." Brooke writhed helplessly between the car and his unforgiving grip. *Say something more. Make up something. Get out of here!* "Peggy has a doctor's appointment that we forgot about, so I came by to pick her—"

"Shut up!" His grip tightened around her throat, cutting off her words. The brown in his right eye swirled as he stuck his face close enough to hers that she felt his spittle on her chin. While a non-panicked part of her brain noted that he wore contacts, and the darkness of his eyes was as fake as the color of his hair, Brooke felt his rock-hard thigh push its way between hers as he lifted her by the neck. Pinpoints of light danced across her vision, but every sickening physical sensation was perfectly clear. "I thought I could do this the easy way. That I wouldn't have to hurt any of you."

"I vote for not hurting!" Louise pounded the inside of the window behind Brooke. "Let go of her! Peggy's calling the police."

"And I liked you three bitches." Brooke sucked in a reviving gulp of air as he released her throat. But it was only to slide his hand down the front of her blouse and curl his fingers beneath the collar. *Oh, God.*

"Tony!" Louise was shouting again. "We believed in you. We gave you a second chance."

He ripped the crinkled cotton of Brooke's blouse. The pearl-white buttons bounced across the pavement as he opened the front of her shirt and traced the chain of her necklace across her sternum and over the swell of her breast. Bile churned in her gut. If his arms were unmarked by tattoos, she could well believe he'd been the man holding that dead, battered woman in the e-mail photograph. She could believe he'd done that to her.

He caught the necklace in his fingers. "Give this to me."

Brooke nodded. "Just get off me. Please."

She could hear Peggy on the phone now, and sirens in the distance. Maybe it was a trick of wishful thinking to think her call had already summoned help. Maybe these few seconds pinned against her car really were lasting for the eons they felt like.

"Please." She wasn't above begging for her freedom.

Tony rubbed his body against hers with a threatening familiarity before backing off an inch or two to allow her to free her hands to unfasten the chain around her neck. She unhooked the clasp and gathered the chain and charm and key in her palm.

Brooke wasn't above tricking the SOB, either.

She held out the prize he wanted. Then dropped it to the pavement.

"You ugly bitch."

The instant Tony bent down to retrieve the necklace, Brooke slipped to the side, wrapped her fingers around the door handle and jerked it open, smacking Tony's shoulder and knocking him on his backside.

The moment he took to curse was the moment she took to snatch up the necklace and dive into the front seat and close the door behind her. With the hem of her skirt caught inside the door, she twisted around to turn the key in the ignition. "Come on. Come on!"

An explosion of sound roared beside her ear and shook the car. Brooke screamed.

"Help us!" Peggy shouted into the phone.

Horns honked around them. The sirens grew louder. Someone was trying to help.

"Give me the damn key!"

Brooke watched Tony's face redden through the spider web of splintering cracks at her side window. He raised the heavy pot and drew it back to strike again.

"Start the car!" Louise yelled.

His aim was off with the second blow. This time he hit more metal than glass and the pot shattered.

"Brooke!"

"I need that key!"

The entire car rocked as Tony lowered his shoulder to the frame and shoved.

Peggy dropped the phone and grabbed on to the dash-board and door as the car leaned toward a forty-five degree angle. "He's going to tip us over!"

Louise slid across the back seat. "Hold on!"

Brooke yanked her skirt up to her thighs and freed her leg to stomp on the clutch. She turned the key and the engine roared to life. She reached for the gearshift.

But it was too late.

Tony bellowed in triumph as the tiny car flipped onto its side. Someone screamed. More glass shattered. The silk skirt ripped as gravity dragged Brooke over the center console.

She tried to tear her skirt the rest of the way to free herself and find her feet so she could move. "Peggy?" Her aunt was holding her head. Blood seeped between her fingers. "Louise, are you all right back there?"

"I'm fine. Peggy's hurt."

The car door opened above them. Brooke tumbled back into Peggy. Her aunt groaned. "I'm sorry. I'm so sorry."

A shadow fell over them. "You'll be sorry. Now give me the damn key."

"On the ground, Fierro!" Tony froze in the opening above her. "I said, get on the ground!"

Atticus?

A black steel gun pressed into Tony's temple.

"On the ground. Now."

Deeply pitched. Perfectly articulated. Absolutely deadly with intent.

Fear gave way to pure, unadulterated relief. "Atticus?"

"Are you all right, Brooke?" She still couldn't see his face, but his voice was clear and wonderful to hear.

"I'm fine." Feeling safe enough to think about something

beyond survival for the moment, Brooke braced herself off of Peggy and peeled off her own tattered blouse. "But Peggy's hurt. She hit her head. We need an ambulance."

Tony had lost a contact sometime during the skirmish, and one colorless, albino eye glared down at her before he raised his hands and climbed off the car. Brooke quickly shifted her attention to her injured aunt, balling up her blouse and pressing it to the gash at Peggy's temple.

"I'm so sorry I didn't see Tony for what he was," Brooke apologized.

Louise huddled behind her, rubbing Brooke's back and gently smoothing the hair off her sister's forehead. "It's not your fault, dear. We liked him, too. It's a good person who expects the best in others."

Brooke shook her head. "Only naive idiots think that way."

Peggy blinked her eyes open. "This isn't your fault. You wanted to help him. We all did. It's not…" Her eyes squeezed shut as she groaned in pain.

"Atticus!"

He was at the open door, reaching down for her as she scrambled to her feet. "I'm right here, honey. Come on."

His eyes were lined with some strange emotion that left his eyes dark, like steel. But the no-nonsense grip on her hand was familiar. His easy, comforting strength was the same as he lifted her from the car and down onto the pavement beside him.

She caught a glimpse of Tony Fierro, facedown on the asphalt, with Kevin Grove's knee in his back while the big detective handcuffed him. She almost got a full look at the circle of onlookers crowding around the two SUVs with flashing lights blocking off the scene. But almost as soon as she became aware of the hot sun on her bare shoulders and back, Atticus was wrapping his suit jacket around her and tucking her up against his chest.

"Did he hurt you?" She felt his lips in the crown of her hair, against her cheek, her neck as he bent his head to her shoulder and hugged her close. Brooke snuck her arms around his waist and held on just as tight. "Honey? Are you hurt?"

When she didn't answer, his hands began to squeeze, to move, to push her away as they roamed over her from hair to waist, inspecting her for injury.

"I'm fine." Brooke caught his hands and stopped his search. She looked up into the grim set of his face and laid a palm against his cheek, sensing something barely controlled inside him that needed to be gentled. "Maybe a few scrapes and bruises, but I'm all right." She turned her face back to the car, feeling the anxiety curdling in her stomach again. "But Peggy…"

He nodded, pulled her hand from his face and kissed her palm. "I'll take care of her."

Finding as much comfort in that promise as she had in the circle of his strength and warmth, Brooke slipped her arms into the sleeves of his jacket and clutched it together at her throat. She watched him stride back to the car, his gun tucked in at the back of his waist, his movements quick and confident as he climbed down into the overturned car. With the assistance of a couple of nursery employees, he helped Louise climb out, and then carefully lifted Peggy to safety. He carried Peggy to the front seat of his SUV and covered her with a blanket.

In only a matter of minutes, it seemed, Detective Grove was driving off with a sulking, cursing Tony Fierro locked in the backseat. An ambulance had arrived and Peggy was strapped onto a gurney while Louise and Brooke held her hands. The EMT's report was reassuring. Possibly a concussion. But a few stitches and a night of observation at the hospital were probably all the treatment she would require.

"I love you, sweetie." Peggy was smiling as she was loaded into the ambulance and Louise climbed in beside her. "I've got hardheaded Hansford genes. I'll be fine."

"I know you will. I love you both."

The instant Brooke stepped back, Atticus was there, standing behind her. One hand took hold of hers while the other rested protectively, possessively, at her shoulder. Brooke smiled and turned, seeking his full embrace. "How did you and Detective Grove find us so fast?"

His arms folded around her, welcoming her. "You weren't where you were supposed to be. You didn't show up at the bank at one, so we came looking for you. McCarthy told us you were here."

Before the EMTs closed the doors, Brooke snuggled close, blushing against Atticus's steady heartbeat as she listened to her dear aunts' familiar chatter. "He reminds me of that British diplomat I went out with that time I visited Leo in Sarajevo. Cultured. Take charge. Completely devastating. I definitely like Detective Kincaid better than that other friend of hers."

"Hush, Louise. Apparently, Brooke does, too."

WITH PEGGY napping and Louise unpacking her overnight bag on the guest bed in the hospital room beside her, Brooke finally slipped out of the room and dragged herself down to the waiting room at the end of the hall. Atticus stood up as soon as she entered, and the crick of mild whiplash in her neck seemed instantly to improve.

"How's Peggy?" Despite the loosened tie and collar that indicated he'd been working, she felt like a frump again, sporting a shapeless green hospital shirt while he still wore his suit. The tailored cut of his jacket fitted his broad shoulders better than they'd draped over hers, but she missed the warmth and scent of him around her.

"Resting comfortably. The forms are all complete and there's nothing more I can do until the doctor checks her out in the morning." In spite of her fatigue, Brooke couldn't help but smile. "Besides, you'd think Louise was the practical, down-to-earth sister, the way she's stepping up to take care of Aunt Peg. They don't need me underfoot right now."

"You never know what a person can do until they're called upon to do it." Atticus plucked a tendril of hair from the temple of her glasses and brushed it behind her ear. "Like a woman taking on a man who weighs twice as much as she does, with nothing more than guts to protect herself with."

His compliment warmed her as much as his gentle touch. "It was a good thing we could lock ourselves in the car."

"Good thing, hell." He curled his fingers into his palm and pulled away. "I saw that car go over when I pulled into the parking lot. I thought…" He took a moment to button his collar, straighten his tie and bury the thought. "Cars are usually Holden's thing, but next time you go shopping for one, I'm going with you to make sure you choose something heavy enough that not even a superhero can get to you inside."

"Superhero?" Brooke pressed her lips together to hide her smile. Perhaps Atticus had had as good a fright as she had. But it was a secret she'd let him keep. "I'm just glad you came along when you did. Once Tony got the door open, I kind of ran out of ideas." The image of his red, angry face, so determined to take something from her, wiped away the urge to smile. The hospital really did have its air conditioning cranked on high this afternoon. "Tony's locked up, right?"

Atticus must have noticed the goose bumps on her arms, or the way she couldn't quite hug herself tightly enough to stay warm. He reached out and rubbed his hands up and down her arms. "I doubt he'll ever be a free man again. Grove booked him on assault and battery, and is questioning him about Dad's murder. He claims he has a track record of sexual harassment, but that somebody set him up to make it look as though he was stalking you. I just got off the phone with Grove. Fierro still won't say boo about his expunged record, and he claims he doesn't even know who my father was. He's not talking."

Brooke pulled her necklace from the V-neck of her shirt. "He may not have to once we find out what secrets this key unlocks."

"Grove was anxious for answers about that, too. I was glad to have the backup this afternoon." But maybe not so glad that she'd told Detective Grove just how involved she and Atticus had been in investigating John Kincaid's murder? She worried her lip between her teeth and let him keep talking. "I'll drive you home to get cleaned up and get a change of clothes. I made arrangements to have your car towed to a repair shop. The nursery will deliver your purchases tomorrow morning. And I called Major Taylor and advised him that you'd be gone for the rest of the day."

"No." If they were going to risk his badge and her life, then they were going to go all the way. "Take me to the bank first. They'll still be open for another half hour." Brooke held up the key. "Tony nearly killed us for this— I want to find out why it's so important."

"Shoot." Brooke's weary sigh whispered against Atticus's eardrums like a mournful cry. "It's just not working."

Still, she somehow found the energy to look over to the foot of the unfinished stairs where he was pacing and brighten the entire place with one of her smiles.

"How did it go with Edward?" Brooke asked.

No way in hell was he going to let her wind up like the dead woman in the photograph Major Taylor had had Marcus Henry send to his phone after hearing of the attack at the nursery parking lot. Tony Fierro was a lucky man that Atticus and Kevin Grove had gotten to him *before* he'd seen the message that bastard had put in her e-mail to terrorize her. He wouldn't have settled for handcuffing him.

"It went." Atticus tore himself away from thoughts of retribution and hung up the phone after talking to his oldest brother. "Ed's on his way to Mom's."

It hadn't been easy, but he'd finally convinced him to drive over to their mother's house to stay the night. He'd already recruited Holden to camp out at the hospital with Peggy and Louise, and Sawyer had his own family to watch.

Nobody he cared about was going to be alone tonight.

Before he walked through the door of Brooke's home this evening, Truman McCarthy had handed him two listening devices that he'd found hooked into the house's wiring so that someone could eavesdrop on Brooke and her aunts. Pretty sophisticated technology—in the same un-usual, hard-to-track and very pricey range of disintegrat-ing bullets. Whatever Tony Fierro had been after, someone else was after, too. They thought Brooke had what they wanted, so that put her in danger—and that meant Atticus wasn't going anywhere.

And if there was a connection between dissolving bullets, violent ex-cons and encrypted disks, then Brooke might not be the only one in danger. With Holden, Sawyer and him all on unofficial duty, he had to turn to big brother to make sure their mother stayed safe as well.

Grief and guilt and alcohol had taken Edward Kincaid to a very dark place. But all four sons loved their mother, and with John Kincaid gone, they couldn't trust anyone else to protect her the way their father would have. At least, that was the argument he had used. And despite some well-chosen expletives about how Atticus could talk his ear off, the argument had worked.

All of Atticus's family was safe for now. All he had to worry about tonight was the klutzy brainiac with the killer legs who seemed almost more determined than he was to uncover whatever was written on that disk.

"That's good. I know you were worried about her. I think it's good for Edward, too, not to be alone so much."

"Yeah." He crossed the room and dropped his phone into the pocket of his discarded jacket on the granite-top island where he'd removed his tie, badge and holster. "I don't think he can stand the thought of losing anyone else. He may make for lousy company, but he'll take care of Mom well enough."

Looking wearied by even that brief conversation,

Brooke set her glasses on the makeshift table he'd made
for her out of an unfinished door and two sawhorses. She
leaned back in the metal folding chair and pinched the
bridge of her nose between her fingers. The night was
black outside the locked church windows. The air inside
was still and stifling. And she'd been staring at the screen
of her laptop computer for three hours straight.

He felt like enough of a heel, allowing her to set up a
mini-office in the middle of the construction zone she lived
in, and work all evening. But one thing he was learning
about Brooke Hansford was that shy didn't mean weak,
and it didn't mean she couldn't be stubborn as hell.

He'd admire that tenacity in any partner he worked with.
He admired it in her.

But enough was enough. For now. She'd showered and
changed into a paint-stained tank top and cut-off shorts.
And with her damp hair curling up around her shoulders,
she looked young and fragile. And though one part of him
was fighting the temptation brought on by seeing so much
creamy skin exposed by the modest outfit, another part of
him was hating the bruises forming purple and red marks
at her collarbone and dappling across her back, arms and
legs. He should have gotten there sooner today. He never
should have let Tony Fierro put his hands on her.

"Why don't you take a break?" he suggested, needing
a break himself from the guilt and worry eating him up
inside. "Rest your eyes and clear your head. I can make you
a fresh glass of iced tea."

"No, thanks." It wasn't that she'd drunk enough tea, but
that she refused to give up trying to crack the encryption
code on the disk they'd found in his father's secret lockbox.

"Who'd have thought? As much as your dad loathed computers, he knew enough to create several layers of security on this disk. Every time I get through one code, another one springs up to take its place." She leaned forward, probably so she could read the screen without her glasses. "It's too complicated—as if the code itself is some kind of diversion."

Atticus pulled up one of the stools from the kitchen area and sat beside her. "Could it be something simpler? A single name or number?"

"I thought that might be the case, too." Her shoulders lifted with another sigh, then hitched. Her fingers went to her neck to massage the ache she must be feeling there. Before he could judge whether it was a wise idea or not, Atticus moved behind her and placed his hands there instead.

Her skin was warm to the touch, and every bit as velvety smooth as it looked. She tensed at the unexpected touch, but Atticus wasn't sure he had the strength to pull away. Just the simple touch of his fingertips to her shoulders sent a warm sluice of heat from the point of contact to the roiling worries inside him, taking the edge off those sharp emotions. "Is this okay?" he asked.

Brooke hesitated, then nodded. When she closed her eyes and leaned back into his massage, the turbulence inside him seemed to relax as well.

He barely pressed into her muscles as he moved along her neck and down her arms, not wanting to aggravate any minor injury. Instead, he simply stroked and rubbed, relying on the friction between them to create a soothing heat.

A minute or two passed and he felt her begin to loosen up before she spoke again. "I've tried his name, your mother's name, your brothers', his street address and birth date. The disk just throws up another wall and won't let me in."

"It'll come to you, honey. Between the two of us, we'll figure out what Dad had to say."

She blinked her eyes open, revealing their clear, verdant beauty. But just as he was struck by the glimpse of their tranquil loveliness, she pulled away from him and reached for her glasses.

"I can't quit now. Your dad was counting on me to figure it out. *You're* counting on me. I don't want to disappoint either of you."

"Hey." He lifted her fingers from the keyboard and clicked on the icon to eject the disk. "I think I'm speaking for Dad as well as myself when I say that there is no way in hell you could ever disappoint us."

"But—"

"No buts." He batted her fingers away from the disk and placed it back in its plastic case. After securing the disk inside his jacket pocket, he took her hand and pulled her to her feet. "The best thing for a tired brain and good intentions is a solid night's sleep. Let's get you tucked into bed, and we'll get an early start in the morning."

Grabbing his jacket and gun, Atticus led the way through the unfinished great room to her bedroom, where fresh paint, curtains and a hand-stitched quilt made him think of the warm, wonderful solace Brooke had brought to his life. He walked right past the sleeping bag she'd set outside her door and followed her inside.

"What are you doing?"

He closed the door behind him and looked down into her upturned eyes. "My brain and good intentions are beat, too. If you don't mind, honey, I'd like to be where I can keep an eye on you—and if I should doze off, I can still feel you're with me and that you're safe."

She wrapped her fingers around the curling wrought iron at the foot of her bed. "You…want to sleep with me?"

The wide-eyed surprise of that innocent question triggered a wry smile. He was probably setting himself up for a tortuous challenge to his self-control because he could bet that she squirmed and cuddled when she slept the same way she hugged and held on to a man when she was awake.

But he was determined to be a gentleman about this. "Let's say you crawl under the covers and I'll sleep on top. But I can still hold you if that's all right."

"You *don't* want to sleep with me?"

The chagrin that made her voice husky was more potent than any of Hayley's calculated seductions had been. His tired body suddenly awakened with possibilities. How could he have never known how much he wanted this woman? But he ignored the zing of anticipation and hung his jacket on the door, and moved around her to set his gun on the table between the bed and window.

He pulled off his belt and untucked the tails of his shirt. "Now that's a loaded question, honey."

"*Honey.* Why do you keep calling me that?"

Had he? So now endearments were slipping out? How did he think he was going to be able to maintain control of his baser urges when she was warm and sweet and snuggled against him in the middle of a bed? He couldn't even control those silly, intimate words that a man and woman who were more than mere friends shared.

"Atticus?" He hadn't heard her follow him around the

bed. When she palmed the middle of his back, everything in his body leaped at the innocent touch.

Hell. Control was going to be damn near impossible.

She was already backing away when he spun around. With her head bowed, she beat a hasty retreat around to her side of the bed, misreading his reaction. "I'm sorry. It was just a question. A stupid one. A more experienced woman wouldn't even ask it."

"Brooke."

She opened a dresser drawer and pulled out a mint-green nightshirt and tossed it onto the bed behind her. "I'm sure it doesn't mean anything. I wasn't fishing for a date or something like that. I mean, hell, why would you…? I mean…"

"Brooke." When a pair of matching panties sailed toward his face, Atticus caught them. His decision was made.

"Last night was probably a mistake. And you're just being nice. And—"

"You talk too much."

"Me?" Her sweet, pink lips were open when she turned to face him. "I am the quietest—"

He closed his mouth over Brooke's and stopped her nervous ramblings in the most satisfying way he could imagine.

"I'm…what are…?"

He almost laughed when she tried to keep talking. Almost. But a surrendering sigh, like a purr in her throat, welcomed his kiss and stoked his desire. And when she wound her arms around his neck and angled her mouth so he could deepen the kiss, Atticus reached down to the decadent curve of her bottom and lifted her.

"Hold on to me," he commanded, and was nearly knocked off his feet by his body's fierce response to those gorgeous legs linking behind his back and opening her most feminine heat to his driving need. "Easy, honey. Easy."

"There. You said it." Her jubilant smile against his mouth sent a wild hunger pumping through his veins. She made that crazy tingle at the point of his chin when she nipped him there. He stumbled and had to brace one hand on the wall behind her when she laved her tongue over that same sensitive spot. "You called me honey. What does that mean?"

"It means you're special to me. It means I want to be with you." He rasped the words against the vibrant pulse at the dip beneath her ear. "Never doubt that."

"I want you, too…honey."

The last bit of caution guarding his heart cracked into pieces and was carried away by desire. With her knees hugging his hips, he turned and fell onto the bed with her. He peeled the tank top off, exposing those pert, perfect breasts to his appreciative eyes and hungry mouth. What another man might have found lacking, Atticus treasured. Her nipples were taut and responsive, and whether it was a gentle tweak between his fingers or a greedy pull against his tongue, Brooke panted and purred at every touch.

With his desire straining against his zipper, Atticus reached for the snap of her denim shorts. Her fingers were slower, but no less determined to rid him of his shirt and then the rest of his clothes.

Her wandering hands were wreaking havoc over his naked body when they suddenly stilled and pressed against his chest.

"Atticus, I've never been with a man."

"I kind of guessed that." He braced himself up on an elbow beside her, gently stroking the hair from her face as he studied her kiss-stung lips and the vulnerable tilt of her eyes looking up at him over the top of her glasses. He held himself still against her hip and made her a promise. "If you're not sure I'm the one or you decide you're not ready, tell me. We'll stop. At any time. I don't want to hurt you."

"No. You're definitely the one. Maybe you've always been the one. I'm just not sure…" She pulled her hands away and clutched them over her breasts, leaving his body chilled with their absence. "What am *I* supposed to do? I don't want to just lie here like a lump and have it be awful for you."

He smiled at that. "First, it's *you*, so it could never be awful." He dipped his head and kissed her. "And second, you're a ringer, Miss Hansford. A natural talent in the passion department. Trust your instincts. Keep talking, so I know if it's getting awkward or uncomfortable for you." He stroked his fingers along her delicate jaw. "I have a feeling you'll pick the details up pretty quickly."

"A natural talent?" The hands began to move. Five curious toes curled behind his knee.

"Oh, yeah." Atticus rolled on top of her, letting her body become familiar with his weight and shape. "In so many ways."

He paused a moment to take off her glasses and set them on the bedside table. Anxious fingers dug into his shoulders. "Atticus, I can't see."

She was a resourceful woman. "Then I guess you'll just have to feel your way around."

Brooke's laughter answered his. And then, they were done laughing as she took his advice to heart and began an exploration that left him as breathless as she. After leaving her for a moment to sheath himself, he came back for reassuring eye-to-eye contact before claiming her mouth and sliding inside her. He held himself still as her tight warmth stretched to welcome him. He kissed away her soft gasp and waited for the urging of her fingers against his spine before he began to move and carry them both to an explosive peak that was as new and amazing to him as it was for her before tumbling down the other side together.

Afterward, when she'd fallen asleep against his chest, with no covers, no pajamas, and no hint of regret between them, Atticus lay awake, stroking her hair and reflecting on what had just happened.

His control was shot to hell where Brooke was concerned. He wasn't supposed to care about her this much. But he did. He was supposed to be looking out for her, not taking advantage of her passionate curiosity. But things were already stirring, wanting her again. He was supposed to be the teacher, and she the pupil.

Somehow, in these past few days, Brooke had turned the tables on him. The student had taught him a thing or two about honesty and passion, intimacy and courage. She'd stripped away his cynicism about trust and innocence and taking chances.

He'd never expected to feel deeply about any woman again.

Atticus was a rational man who always liked to stay two or three steps ahead of the other guy. He calculated probabilities and profiled criminals and had a good idea of how almost any person would act in almost any given situation. He reasoned. He planned.

Now he was falling in love with Brooke.

And he'd never seen it coming.

Chapter Twelve

Atticus listened carefully to Kevin Grove's report. He knew the only reason he'd been allowed to sit at this table in this conference room was that Mitch Taylor had ordered him to be a part of this briefing. The official mumbo-jumbo had been something about his *superior investigation skills* and the fact that he'd been in on Tony Fierro's arrest.

He even began to wonder if his new precinct boss was going soft. The team of forensic specialists and veteran detectives sitting around the table were talking about things related to his father's murder—similarities between the deaths of his father, James McBride and the Jane Doe they'd removed from the landfill. Did they think he could provide some insight? Was this really just an unofficial way to keep the Kincaid brothers apprised of the investigation without the D.A.'s office or Internal Affairs pitching a fit about personal bias? Or was he being given this information because it affected Brooke—and Major Taylor was a seasoned enough detective to know when one of his men had taken on the role of bodyguard and lover to his near-sighted administrative assistant?

No. Major Taylor would never go soft. Atticus was here for a reason.

Tony Fierro was dead. Stabbed during the night in lockup.

"Our key witness, Liza Parrish, identified Fierro as the driver of the car she saw leaving the Kincaid murder scene." Detective Grove passed a stack of enlarged photographs around the table. "The first picture is our sketch artist's rendering of the black man she described. You'll note the face is pretty vague, but so was her description. She's fairly sure about his size, though. He stands about six foot three and weighs in at about two hundred twenty pounds. She never heard him speak."

What Atticus had mistaken for dull and plodding in Grove's investigation was really patient and thorough. If Kevin Grove put a case together, it was going to stick. "What about the 'suit' Ms. Parrish says she saw get in the car? Do we have any description on him?"

"I can't even tell you if it is a him. She saw a gray pinstriped jacket and dark hair through a tinted window."

When Atticus flipped to the next picture, he finally understood why he'd been asked to sit in on the meeting. "Son of a bitch."

"See something useful, Kincaid?" Grove asked.

Dr. Holly Masterson, sitting across the table from him recognized it. Mitch Taylor would have understood what was in the picture, too.

It was a photograph of Tony Fierro's body, lying dead on the floor of his cell. And there on the concrete, drawn in blood by his own dying hand, was the number three.

The same number three that had appeared as a microscopic tattoo on three different murder victims.

The number three that Brooke wore on a charm around her neck.

"IT'S A number three. In the blood on the floor and on Fierro's keychain. Just like your charm."

Brooke pulled the gold chain from inside the front of her paint shirt and frowned against the phone. "My charm?"

She heard the revs and honks of rush-hour traffic in the background of Atticus's call. He'd been called into the office for a special meeting and was on his way back to the house where he'd been camping out for the past three nights.

"You said your father gave it to you. That it belonged to your mother."

"That's right." She traced her thumb around the loops carved into the gold. "But it's not a number three carved into my charm."

"Of course, it is. I've seen it."

Brooke turned the gold disk, seeing the design the way someone who hadn't lived with the gift and story that went with it her entire life might. "It looks like a three. But it's a Cyrillic letter. My mother was of Slavic descent. It's a Z. Z for Zorinsky. My mother's maiden name."

Wait a minute. Gold disk. Z for Zorinsky.

Brooke's gaze slid over to the laptop where she'd been working. "Z for Zorinsky," she muttered, thinking out loud.

"Brooke? Are you still there?"

"I'm here." She crossed the room to her sawhorse desk and sat in front of her laptop.

"Put Holden on the line."

She opened the disk and loaded it. "He just left to drive Peggy and Louise to the store to refill Aunt Peg's prescription and get some groceries. I think Peggy wanted to get out after being on bed rest for three days."

Atticus swore. "He's supposed to be there watching you."

"No, he's supposed to be watching Peggy and Louise. *You're* supposed to be watching me." Did that sound like she was sniping at him? She instantly felt contrite. "I mean, I'm not blaming you. You got called in and I need to work on cracking your father's code on this disk. Besides, Tony's in jail and I'm perfectly fine."

"Tony's dead."

"What?" A shiver of unease rippled down her spine.

"He was murdered in his cell last night. That's what the briefing was about." She could almost hear Atticus stepping on the accelerator and passing other vehicles. "Are McCarthy's men there?"

"They don't work on Sundays."

"So you're alone?"

Brooke got up to check the doors and windows. "Don't worry. Everything is locked. I'm right here, sweating away, waiting for you to get here. You are still coming over for dinner, right?"

Or did Tony's death mean he'd lost his reason to keep such a close eye on her? Had they moved too fast with their relationship? Of course, they'd known each other for several years. Not exactly what she'd consider a speedy courtship. But then they'd yet to go out on a real date. In public. Where other people could see that they were together.

She didn't expect Atticus to suddenly become a romantic and start reciting poems and declaring his love, and she certainly didn't want any surprise bouquets of flowers. But she was completely, crazily in love with the man—maybe she had been for years. The threats to her life and spending so much time together had finally peeled away her inhibitions and made second-guessing her feelings and thoughts seem like a wasteful luxury.

She'd fallen hard. But had Atticus?

Unless he presented her with a ring or said the words, how was a woman supposed to know?

"Stop analyzing stuff in your head and doublecheck the locks. I'm on my way there right now."

"Why would I be in danger?" Irrationally disappointed that he could know she was stewing over something, yet not fathom what she was stewing about, she sat back at the desk and clicked on the disk icon. Brooke had to try. She started typing in a word.

Z-O-R...

"Oh, I don't know. Because whoever killed Tony Fierro is probably looking for the same thing he was. That disk you're playing with!"

She wasn't playing anymore. Brooke shot to her feet and shouted.

"I've got it. Atticus, I've got it! I just unlocked your father's disk."

Zorinsky was the key.

She was the key.

Brooke's family name had unlocked John's secrets. That's why he'd left the clues in her journal for her to find. She was a Zorinsky. She would be able to break his code.

The files she'd opened thus far had been all about his

life before becoming a Kansas City police officer some thirty-plus years ago, about his life in military intelligence and his assignment to a covert spy cell he referred to as Z-Group. Z-Group had operated out of the embassies of eastern Europe during the Cold War. John had been recruited as a young man to join a team which had included her mother and father.

John Kincaid was a spy.

Her parents were spies. Past tense.

And John knew why they had died.

Did he also know who had rigged her father's car to crash that fateful day? Did he know his own killer?

The sun outside her home had moved beyond the heat of the day. But Brooke was miles away from Kansas City as she became entranced by the secret life that John Kincaid had wanted her to know about. He was creating a record, and clearing his conscience, she supposed.

And though she still had the majority of the disk's files left to read, she could already imagine that the information contained therein provided more than enough motive for his death.

"Oh, my God. John." Brooke reached beneath her glasses to wipe away the tears as she read the next entry in John Kincaid's encrypted journal.

This one was a letter, actually.

A letter addressed to her.

Brooke—

I don't regret for one moment bringing you into my life. You're a hell of a secretary—but more than that, you're a sweet, beautiful young woman with a kind heart, a sharp mind and more patience than an old fart like me deserves. I'm glad you're part of our lives. You're a true family friend and, I'll say it, you're like a daughter to Su and me.

But I owe you an explanation. I owe you an apology.

I knew you lived in Kansas City with your aunts long before you graduated from high school or college and came to work at the police department. Once I saw your name on the new hires list, I wanted to meet you in person. And once I met you—if memory serves me correctly, it was hot coffee you spilled down my pant leg during that first interview—I knew I wanted to know you better.

I took you under my wing because I felt guilty over Leo and Irina's deaths. We'd worked so closely together in Z-Group that they were like family, too. Your mother was a beautiful woman, a spectacularly resourceful and talented agent (hmm, I wonder where you get your ability to adapt and think on your feet). Your father was a good man and a good friend who sacrificed more than any of us to keep the Soviet bloc from exposing our agents and stealing our secrets.

Your mother turned out to be a double agent— trading our technologies as often as she brought us something useful from behind the Iron Curtain—endangering all our lives and threatening to undermine the entire project. Leo was the one who volunteered to eliminate her. He said he couldn't allow anyone else to take care of his wife. He was so heartbroken.

You have to understand. It was the Cold War. Countries in eastern Europe were revolting against their governments and falling apart. It was impossible to know who to trust beyond our team—Me. Bill Caldwell. James McBride. Leroy Maynard. Charlie Rogers. Laura Zook. Alistair Hunt. Irina and Leo. I'm telling you the names because we were all responsible for your parents' deaths. Leo staged the car accident—I think he wanted all three of you to die so that none of you would have to be alone—but we all agreed that Irina was a threat. We all agreed she had to be taken care of.

Brooke, I've signed documents and taken blood oaths to keep the business of Z-Group and its operatives secret for as long as I live. When the Cold War ended, the need for the cell ended. But the promise remained. The guilt stayed with me, too.

I love you like a daughter, kiddo. And I value your friendship. But I'm partly responsible for your parents' deaths. Someday, I hope you can forgive me for that.

Until then, be healthy, stay safe. And know that you have always been loved.

—John

She didn't remember her mother, but she'd been a traitor. She didn't remember her father, but he'd been a hero.

"Don't let Brooke go with her mother." Brooke sniffled as she repeated her father's last words. After reading John's letter, they took on a whole new meaning than the one she'd been allowed to believe.

Not, *don't let Brooke die.* But rather, *Irina's the enemy. Don't let my daughter be with the enemy.*

Did Leo Hansford even know if his mission to eliminate

his wife—a double agent—had been a success? Had he died fearing that Irina Zorinsky was still a threat to the members of the team? Had he intended to die along with her? Or had his last assignment gone horribly wrong?

Were her parents' deaths and the cover-up that followed the reason John and other members of the defunct Z-Group had been murdered?

Unable to read any more, Brooke closed the file and ejected the disk. Tucking the disk case into the back pocket of her cutoff shorts, she picked up the phone to call Atticus.

And realized she wasn't alone.

Chapter Thirteen

"Mirza?"

Seeing her friend's face topped by a blonde wig and purple K-State ball cap, and scowling at her through the window of her back door seemed almost as incongruous as the large gun pointed at her through the glass.

Brooke didn't wait for the picture to make sense. She debated for all of two nanoseconds whether to climb into the rafters and hide, or get the hell out of there, before spinning around toward the front door. She lurched as the entryway behind her exploded. She never heard the discharge of the gun, but splintered wood and flying glass were bombardment enough to send her tearing through the house.

"I want that disk. I know you found it."

Where was the musical Indian accent? What happened to the timid friend who'd been afraid to leave his cubicle?

She reached the thick oak doors, original to the building. Beautiful to look at, heavy and warped and unwieldy enough for Brooke to curse their fine craftsmanship. She twisted the lock open and tugged at the crossbar. "Come on!"

"Be the smart little girl I know you are and give me the

disk!" Mirza kicked out the jagged glass and reached inside to unlock the door. "I'll make sure your death is swift and painless."

"How about I just don't die at all!" The heavy oak groaned as Brooke scraped the crossbar across its moorings.

Heavy footsteps coming up fast behind her spurred her strength. Brooke smacked into the door as the crossbar popped free and her momentum threw her forward. Pretending the blow to her head wasn't ringing through her entire skull, she swung open the door and ran out into the hazy twilight.

"That disk is mine!" Mirza thundered after her. "I worked too hard to get it." Brooke circled around the house, avoiding the windows and sticking to the spreading shadows. She didn't know if she was heading for a neighbor's house or the open street or a place to hide. She only knew she had to get the disk someplace safe. "I played stupid so I could get close to you. I sent you flowers and messages and copied all of Fierro's bad habits so that the cops would focus their attention on him. We knew you had access to Kincaid's files. I just had to stay close to you until you found it."

We? Mirza and Tony were in this together? No. He was in competition with Tony Fierro, using her association with the ex-con to terrorize her so completely that Mirza could sneak into her world unnoticed. He'd had access to deliver those flowers, that letter. Putting that mutilated picture on her e-mail would have been a cakewalk for a man of Mirza's skills.

So who was the *we* he was talking about?

Survive first. Think later.

Brooke ducked down behind one of McCarthy's

portable generators and wondered if Mirza could hear her deep, labored breathing. *Think, Brooke. Think.* She didn't need to bring a man with a gun into any of her neighbor's houses. Her car was in the shop. Where did she run? Where could she hide?

"I know you're alone, Brooke." Mirza's footsteps crunched on the hard-packed dirt. "I waited until that cop and your aunts left. I know your boyfriend isn't here."

The lumber.

Before Mirza and his gun rounded the corner, Brooke scooted between the stacks of wood waiting to become the second floor of her house. Needing to arm herself, she pried at one of the boards. The long piece jiggled but refused to budge.

The footsteps stopped.

Brooke caught her breath and held it, desperately trying to get a fix on Mirza's position through the pulse beat pounding in her ears.

So much for arming herself. So much for running. She straightened her back against the lumber and slowly inched along her way to the corner. Back… Back…

A hard hand closed over her mouth, muffling Brooke's scream as a man pulled her around the corner.

He pushed her against the lumber, wrapping his body around her like a cocoon. She recognized Atticus by scent alone, even before she heard his toneless whisper.

"Shh. It's me, honey."

But Mirza had already heard the yip of sound and was closing in.

Atticus's lips moved against her ear, sending frissons of warmth to mix with the shivers of fear that left her shaking.

"With that silencer, I'm guessing he only has five or six shots. He's coming from the left. I'll draw him out to the right. If he starts firing wildly, dive for the ground and stay put. I called for backup, but if I go down before they get here, I want you to take my gun and shoot the son of a bitch."

He truly stunk at pep talks.

But Brooke nodded her understanding and clung to the wood as Atticus removed his hand and turned toward the footsteps. His gun was drawn, his arm rock-steady.

Death approached.

"I love you."

Brooke mouthed the words, whispered a prayer.

"Stay put," Atticus ordered before disappearing around the corner.

The eight longest seconds of her life passed by before two seconds of gunfire played out in Brooke's backyard. She dropped to the ground as Atticus had instructed, nearly chewing through her lip to keep herself from shouting out his name. Sulfuric wisps of gunpowder hung in the air and stung her nose. She heard grunts and cursing. A distinctive click and then silence.

How long did she wait before crawling around the corner to see if Atticus was still alive?

A sleek red sports car skidded through the gravel on the street and jumped the curb, grinding to a stop only a few feet from her hiding place. Holden climbed out, gun in hand. Backup had arrived.

Could she move now?

"Brooke!"

Atticus. She was on her feet and running before he called her name a second time.

He was tucking his gun into the back of his belt and straightening his jacket when she launched herself at him. He braced his feet and caught her on the fly. But they still tumbled backward into the stack of lumber. Brooke held on tight and landed safely in his arms. He was alive. He was safe.

He was kissing the stuffing out of her.

Holding her face between hands that meant business, he kissed her again, and again, and again, with a rare abandon that left her feverish and flustered and unable to speak.

"I love you, too, honey. I love you, too."

She was vaguely aware of Holden looming up behind Atticus. "I'd ask if you needed my help, big brother, but I'm afraid I'd get my face slapped."

"The perp's on the ground. I cuffed him to the generator. He's got a bullet graze on his arm. Take care of it."

Holden nodded. "That I can handle." He glanced over Atticus's shoulder and winked at Brooke. "Looks like the situation is under control here."

Holden was gone by the time Atticus let Brooke come up for air. He brushed his thumbs beneath her glasses, wiping away her tears. The exuberance of that out-of-control kiss had faded. "You've been crying."

"I'm tired of solving mysteries and playing detective." She pulled the disk from her back pocket and pushed it into Atticus's hands. "Here. Take it. It's what Mirza was after. It's what Tony wanted, too. It's all about something called Z-Group, involving John and my parents and some other… spies. And I think my mother… may be the reason your father was killed."

Instead of condemnation, she heard admiration in his tone. "You cracked the code."

"I cracked the code." She lifted her gaze up to his steel-gray eyes, needing to see the truth—whatever it might be—written there. "Did you hear me? I think my mother was the reason your father was killed. Some kind of cover-up. Do you still want to say you love me?"

"I love you," he gloated, succinctly enough for her to believe it. Atticus tucked Brooke beneath his chin and she wrapped her arms around his waist and snuggled close. At one of the most unsettled times of her life, this was the safest, warmest—only—place she wanted to be.

"How about this?" Atticus asked, moving so he could kiss her hair, her nose, her lips. "Next time we have a mystery to solve, I'll play the part of the hard-nosed detective, and you play the role of the smart, scrappy—fairly uncoordinated—and absolutely beautiful woman I love."

"That's your best pep talk yet." Brooke smiled and kissed him back.

Epilogue

"Mr. Smith, is it done?"

"Yes. Patel is dead. A tragic mix-up with tainted blood at the hospital where he was being treated. It was far easier to accomplish than your son's death."

The boss swallowed hard, surprised at the twinge of remorse. "Antonio was never my son. He was a bastard child. A mistake."

"And yet you hired him to work for you. How many years did he serve your cause?"

"Twenty-seven. Not counting the ten years he was in prison."

"Twenty-seven years? And you never once admitted to him that you were his—"

"Antonio was a secret I wanted to keep. Just like the disk Patel promised he'd retrieve for me. I actually thought he was going to succeed." Mr. Smith opened the car's door, and climbed in behind the wheel himself before the boss continued. "But now Antonio is dead and I'm left in a little bit of a dicey situation."

"You want me to track down the alledged witness?"

Meeting the dark eyes in the rearview mirror, the boss nodded. Without corroboration from a witness, Kincaid's disk was just the fanciful imagining of a burned-out cop with a big imagination. A motive with no perp. Without the disk, KCPD's mystery witness was just someone who'd seen a car outside an old warehouse. A clue with no context.

But if the KCPD acquired both pieces of the puzzle and someone was bright enough to put them together...

"Find that witness. I want you to take care of it personally. No games this time."

"What about Brooke Hansford and Atticus Kincaid?" Mr. Smith started the engine and pulled the car into Kansas City's downtown traffic. "They just bought two plane tickets to Sarajevo. She wants to bring her father's body to Kansas City and rebury him here."

Dicey was an understatement. Decisive action needed to be taken. "What about her mother?"

"Miss Hansford has clearance to dig up her mother's body, too. I'm sure they're trying to confirm the KCPD's double-agent theory, and how John Kincaid was going to blow the whistle on events that went down thirty years ago." Mr. Smith was proving to be just as thorough as each of his predecessors had been. "What happens if she decides to run DNA tests on the remains in that casket?"

"Then she'll find out that Irina Zorinsky isn't buried there."

* * * * *

The Kincaid brothers' investigation
continues this October in
PRIVATE S.W.A.T. TAKEOVER,
only from Harlequin Intrigue.

REQUEST YOUR FREE BOOKS!

2 FREE NOVELS
PLUS 2
FREE GIFTS!

⬧ HARLEQUIN®

INTRIGUE®

Breathtaking Romantic Suspense

YES! Please send me 2 FREE Harlequin Intrigue® novels and my 2 FREE gifts (gifts are worth about $10). After receiving them, if I don't wish to receive any more books, I can return the shipping statement marked "cancel." If I don't cancel, I will receive 6 brand-new novels every month and be billed just $4.24 per book in the U.S. or $4.99 per book in Canada, plus 25¢ shipping and handling per book and applicable taxes, if any*. That's a savings of close to 15% off the cover price! I understand that accepting the 2 free books and gifts places me under no obligation to buy anything. I can always return a shipment and cancel at any time. Even if I never buy another book from Harlequin, the two free books and gifts are mine to keep forever.

182 HDN EEZ7   382 HDN EEZK

Name	(PLEASE PRINT)	
Address		Apt. #
City	State/Prov.	Zip/Postal Code

Signature (if under 18, a parent or guardian must sign)

Mail to the **Harlequin Reader Service:**
IN U.S.A.: P.O. Box 1867, Buffalo, NY 14240-1867
IN CANADA: P.O. Box 609, Fort Erie, Ontario L2A 5X3

Not valid to current subscribers of Harlequin Intrigue books.

Want to try two free books from another line?
Call 1-800-873-8635 or visit www.morefreebooks.com.

* Terms and prices subject to change without notice. N.Y. residents add applicable sales tax. Canadian residents will be charged applicable provincial taxes and GST. Offer not valid in Quebec. This offer is limited to one order per household. All orders subject to approval. Credit or debit balances in a customer's account(s) may be offset by any other outstanding balance owed by or to the customer. Please allow 4 to 6 weeks for delivery. Offer available while quantities last.

Your Privacy: Harlequin is committed to protecting your privacy. Our Privacy Policy is available online at www.eHarlequin.com or upon request from the Reader Service. From time to time we make our lists of customers available to reputable third parties who may have a product or service of interest to you. If you would prefer we not share your name and address, please check here. ☐

HI08R

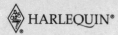

HARLEQUIN®

INTRIGUE®

COMING NEXT MONTH

#1077 THE SHERIFF'S SECRETARY by Carla Cassidy
Sheriff Lucas Jamison and secretary Mariah Harrington had always butted heads. But with her son's life in danger, Mariah trusts the sheriff to uncover a kidnapper hiding in their peaceful community—no matter the secrets revealed.

#1078 DANGEROUSLY ATTRACTIVE by Jenna Ryan
With a killer terrorizing police detective Vanessa Connor, Rick Maguire was assigned to protect her. But the enticing federal agent had to lead her further into danger if she was ever to be safe again.

#1079 A DOCTOR-NURSE ENCOUNTER by Carol Ericson
A relationship between Nurse Lacey Kirk and Dr. Nick Marino had always been expressly forbidden. But nothing could keep them apart amidst a string of deadly cover-ups and patients with secret identities.

#1080 UNDER SUSPICION, WITH CHILD by Elle James
The Curse of Raven's Cliff
Pregnant and alone, Jocelyne Baker believed her love life had been cursed. Yet only fate could have led her into the arms of Andrei Lagios. The cop wore away her defenses, even as the rest of the town grew wary of Jocelyne's return to town.

#1081 BENEATH THE BADGE by Rita Herron
The Silver Star of Texas: Cantara Hills Investigation
Nothing mattered more to Hayes Keller than the badge he wore. But while protecting heiress Taylor Landis, the heart of a real man in need of a good woman was soon exposed.

#1082 BODYGUARD FATHER by Alice Sharpe
Skye Brother Babies
Garrett Skye had a habit of taking on bad assignments, and now he was on the run. But he wasn't willing to leave his baby daughter behind, and that meant taking a stand with teacher Annie Ryder at his side.

www.eHarlequin.com

HICNM0708